# Complete Guide to Greek Mythology for Young and Old

FLORA J. COOKE

Published by A. J. Cornell Publications

ISBN: 978-0-9850501-5-3

# CONTENTS

# 1 OVERVIEW OF GREEK MYTHOLOGY

Hundreds and hundreds of years ago, when Greece and other nations of the world were in their infancy, there were many questions for which people could find no answers. There were no works on astronomy to explain to them that the sunrise is not a real rising of the sun, but is caused by the turning of the earth on its axis; or that the coming of winter after summer is a natural effect of natural causes, and not the work of some malignant power. There were no works on geology to tell of the slow upbuilding of the world through thousands and hundreds of thousands of years; no works on physics to explain that an echo is not an answering voice, but the same voice thrown back by some obstruction. But all of these were natural questions, and the inquiring minds of those primitive people must have satisfaction, so they made up answers and wove them into some of the most beautiful stories and fancies the world has ever known.

This does not mean that some wise man simply invented, all at once, the explanation of such a marvel, for instance, as the sun, with its rising and setting. The explanation grew up gradually. So wonderful an object, which made the whole world bright when it appeared in the east and left the whole world dark when it disappeared in the west, must be more than human; and thus there grew up the idea that the sun was a god—one of the strongest of the gods. Even a god could not walk across the great stretch of the sky between morning and evening, so be was given a chariot with two, four, or six horses. True, his face and form could not be seen, but that was because his chariot, his raiment, and his crown were so brilliant. In time such stories grouped themselves about almost every natural object: the rustling of the leaves was but the murmuring voice of the goddess who lived in the tree; the hurrying stream was a nymph rushing to join her lover, the sea; the stars were virtuous people placed by the gods in the sky that their virtues might never be forgotten. And the sum of these stories, which any people built up for itself, is its *mythology*.

## CLASSES OF MYTHS

Many of the legends and myths were of this kind, answering natural questions about natural objects, and these are known as *explanatory* myths. But there are others that have no such object—which seem, indeed, to have no object but to entertain—and these are called *aesthetic* myths. They tell of the doings of gods and heroes—marvelous doings, often, which prove that however strong the gods may have been, they were not always very good. Such stories as that of Zeus in pursuit of Europa, or of Jason in search of the Golden Fleece, are of this kind.

## WHY STUDY MYTHOLOGY?

Why should learned men, with the knowledge of the world at their fingers' ends, interest themselves in these old fables and legends? What is there to be gained from such study? Much, they tell us, that can be gained in no other way, for the mythology of a people makes clear its ideals, its attitude toward natural happenings, and much about its state of civilization and mode of life. For a *mythology is the religion of a primitive people,* and its science and literature as well. To be sure, those words cannot be taken in just their modern meaning. The old myths were a religion because they set forth the doings of the gods and told the people what worship and sacrifices and ceremonies the gods demanded of them; but in other ways they were very unlike a religion as that word is commonly understood today. For one thing, the gods whom these myths centered about would seem to the modern mind very unfit to be deities, for they were not only jealous and cruel and vengeful, but actually immoral as well. There is a very long word that scholars apply to this sort of a religion—*anthropomorphism;* but it is not a difficult word. It is taken from a Greek word signifying the *human form,* and simply means the attributing of human form and qualities to a divine being.

Then, too, a religion in the modern sense of the term is supposed to try to better people morally, but few of the old mythologies made any such attempt. An ancient Greek, for instance, might lie and steal, but so long as he offered his homage to the gods, and had certain qualities of character, such as courage, he was all right in their sight. Indeed, there was one powerful god, Hermes, who had special charge of thieves and helped them out of their difficulties.

As for science, mythology has a right to that name only in the sense referred to above. It did not, as a modern science does, try to trace effects from causes or work backward to causes from visible effects; it contented itself with assigning supernatural causes to natural events.

Because of the light it throws on all these phases of ancient life, scholars find mythology worthy of study; but the ordinary reader need not go so far for his reason. It is interesting— that is enough; and any child who loves fairy tales cannot fail to be fascinated by these stories woven in the morning of the world when everything was as fresh, as untried, as unexplained to the wisest man as it is to the little child today.

## MYTHS REGARDING THE CREATION OF THE WORLD

One of the questions that demanded an answer was that of the beginning of all things. Anything so wonderful as a world could not just happen, these early peoples believed— some strong power must have made it. Their explanations are interesting.

First of all, said the Greeks, there was just a vast abyss, known as Chaos. From this there rose Love, which created the goddess Gaea (Earth), and from these two came the sky and the mountains, the sea and the animals. Chaos also brought forth two gloomy creatures, Erebus (Darkness) and Nyx (Night), and from these, strangely enough, sprang two beautiful beings, light and day. Gaea bore to Uranus (Heaven) twelve children who grew to gigantic stature and were called Titans. Uranus, first ruler of all things, proved very despotic, and at length Cronus, one of the Titans, with the aid of his mother, dethroned Uranus, and made himself king instead. His period of rule, during which everybody and everything on earth was good and happy, was called the Golden Age, but it did not last. For Zeus, one of Cronus's sons, overthrew him and made himself supreme head of the universe, allotting to his brother Poseidon the sea and to his brother Hades the underworld.

## MYTHS EXPLAINING THE MAKING OF MAN

For a time the gods had the earth to themselves, but it was a lonesome place. Then one day the Titan Prometheus, working with the clay of which he was so fond, molded a figure in the image of the gods, and breathed into it life. Very proud of this creature of his skill, Prometheus wanted to bestow upon him sonic helpful gift, but his brother Epimetheus had used up all the good qualities the animals. To the tortoise had been given hard shell, to the hare swiftness, to the fox slyness and cleverness, to the bear strength, to the tiger fierceness; and what remained for man? Prometheus knew of something more valuable than any of these, and visiting the abode of the gods he brought back with him in a tube that wonderful thing, fire. The gods were very angry, and punished Prometheus and the race of men severely.

## THE MYTHS OF SIN AND PUNISHMENT

The early Greeks saw evil all about them, and they were at a loss to account for it. If the gods made the world, and made it good, where did sin and suffering come from?

In the Golden Age all men were innocent, but they were not to be allowed to escape the vengeance of the gods because they had learned how to use the most wonderful thing the gods themselves possessed—fire. So Pandora, the first mortal woman, was sent with her box, and as a result unhappiness spread through the world. Men became greedy and lustful, hating their brothers, and finally the world became so wicked that Zeus saw that he must sweep it clean of its inhabitants and give it a new, fair start. He caused a great rain to fall and a flood to cover the whole earth, and when it passed, only Deucalion and Pyrrha, virtuous servants of the gods, were left. They were instructed to cast over their shoulders the stones that lay on the mountaintop about them, and the stones turned into humans to repopulate the earth. Is it not strange and interesting to find, in this mythology of the Greeks, a story so very similar to the Biblical account of the Deluge? It is like meeting, in a faraway land where everything is new, one's next-door neighbor.

## THE GODS

The great gods, according to the Greek poets, had their home on Olympus, where they lived in splendor. Zeus was their king, and Hera, his sister and wife, their queen; and the others who had the right to live on this mountaintop were Athena, Apollo, Artemis, Aphrodite, Hermes, Ares, Hephaestus, and Hestea. Demeter, a sister of Zeus, and the goddess of agriculture, had a home on Olympus, but preferred to live on earth, close to her work. There were many, many other deities, some of them, like Eros, with considerable power, while others had jurisdiction only over the particular stream or tree or mountain that was their dwelling place.

# 2 MYTHOLOGICAL GODS, GODDESSES, HEROES, PLACES, AND THINGS

## ACHATES

Achates was one of the Trojans who followed Aeneas and remained with him through all his wanderings and his struggles after the hurried flight from Troy. He was so devoted to Aeneas and so constant that he was always called *fidus* (faithful), and the expression *fidus Achates* has come to be a common one for a very faithful friend.

## ACHILLES

The *Iliad* opens with an account of the wrath of this great Greek hero—"ruinous wrath, which laid unnumbered woes on the Grecians." Achilles was the son of Peleus and the sea-goddess Thetis. Having been well trained in the arts of war, when the Trojan War broke out he joined the Greek army, and during the early years of that struggle he was of great help to the Greeks. However, when Agamemnon, leader of the expedition, took from him Briseis, a captive maiden, he refused to have anything further to do with the war, and the Greeks soon were in desperate straits. Only the death of his beloved friend and kinsman Patroclus made Achilles forget his personal grievances. Filled with the desire for revenge, he rejoined his warring countrymen and turned the tide of their fortunes by slaying Hector, the bravest of the Trojans. According to the early myth-writers, Achilles had been dipped by his mother in the river Styx, which made invulnerable every part of his body except his heel, by which she held him. His death-wound, made by an arrow, he received in this heel.

## ACTAEON
Actaeon was a great hunter and a worshiper of the goddess Artemis. Having by chance come upon the virgin goddess while she was bathing, for his boldness he was changed by her into a stag, despite his protests of innocence. His dogs, not recognizing him, set upon him and tore him to pieces.

## ADONIS
Adonis was a beautiful youth loved by Aphrodite. This goddess, refusing to be consoled after his death, begged Persephone to let him return to the earth from the lower world. The goddess of the lower regions at length consented that the boy should live eight months of each year on earth. This was one of the myths of the seasons, Adonis's months on earth representing the spring,

summer, and early autumn, his months below the ground the gloomy winter.

## AEGIS
The aegis was the shield fashioned by Hephaestus, which Zeus was thought to shake when it thundered, and which Athena carried as a sign of her authority whenever entrusted with a mission by her father. It is frequently mentioned in the *Odyssey* and the *Iliad* and is described in legends as having the head of the Medusa for its center.

## AENEAS
Aeneas was one of the most famous heroes of ancient legend, a Trojan warrior who was second only to Hector in the part he played in the Trojan War. He was the son of Aphrodite and of Anchises, and was chosen to lead a band of followers to a new land in Italy, and there to found a new nation. The story of his wanderings after the fall of Troy is told in Vergil's *Aeneid*.

## AEOLUS
Aeolus was a Greek god to whom was assigned the troublesome task of caring for the winds. His boisterous charges were shut up in a cave in the Aeolion Islands, and a noisy, breezy place it was. According to some accounts he might release them as he wished, but others declared that he could do it only at the command of Poseidon. His name was given to the Aeolian harp.

## AESCULAPIUS

Aesculapius was the god of the art of healing, son of Apollo and the nymph Coronis. When a youth he was placed in care of the centaur Chiron, who taught him what he knew of medicine. Aesculapius, according to the legend, became so versed in his art that he could restore the dead to life. This angered Hades, the insatiable lord of the underworld, and at his request Zeus slew the god of medicine with a thunderbolt. Aesculapius is represented in art as bearing a knotted staff; around this was entwined a serpent, which the ancients regarded as the symbol of health.

## AGAMEMNON

Agamemnon was one of the outstanding figures in ancient Greek legend, brother of Menelaus, whose wife Helen was the cause of the Trojan War. As king of Mycenae and Argos, and thus the most powerful ruler in Greece, Agamemnon was chosen to command all the Greek forces when the struggle commenced. On his return from the war he was killed by his wife Clytemnestra and her lover Aegisthus.

## AJAX

Two of the legendary Grecian heroes in the Trojan War were named Ajax. The son of Telamon, king of Cyprus, was known as the Greater or the Telamonian Ajax, and the son of Oileus, the king of Locris, was called the Lesser or the Locrian Ajax. The Greater was the commander of twelve ships and was called by Homer the bravest of the Greeks except Achilles. In the combat between Odysseus and Ajax for the arms of Achilles after the latter's death, the prize was awarded to Odysseus. The disappointment of Ajax drove him mad, and after slaying all of the sheep of the Greeks, thinking they were the enemy, he killed himself.

The boastful and quarrelsome Ajax the Lesser was a rival of Achilles in swiftness of foot. As a punishment for his brutal treatment of Cassandra after the fall of Troy, it is said that his ship was wrecked and he was struck by lightning.

## ALCESTIS

Alcestis was the wife of Admetus (king of Thessaly) and one of the most attractive characters that have been handed down by legend. An oracle had declared that her husband, whom she loved devotedly, was to die unless someone could be found who would meet Death in his place. His aged father and mother were asked to sacrifice themselves for him, but they refused, and Alcestis finally took upon herself the task of saving him. He pleaded with her not to insist upon her unselfish act, but she was firm, and as Admetus recovered Alcestis died. Hercules (Heracles), however, having pity upon Admetus, met Death at the tomb, vanquished him and brought Alcestis back to life. The *Alcestis* of Euripides is one of the greatest ancient dramas that have been preserved. Browning's *Balaustion's Adventure* is a free translation of it.

## AMAZONS

The Amazons were a race of warlike women who, according to ancient Greek tradition, either permitted no men to reside among them, or kept them in a state of slavery. They are generally supposed to have inhabited the region on the banks of the river Thermodon, in Asia Minor. The most notable city established by them was Ephesus, where they built magnificent temples for the worship of Ares and Artemis. The Amazons were defeated by Hercules, who sought the girdle of their queen Hippolyta; later when leading their armies to the help of Troy, the Amazonian queen was slain by Achilles. The race was finally exterminated by Theseus and the Athenians. It is said that the Amazons burned off their right breast that it might not impede them in the use of the bow; old sculptures, however, do not show such mutilation. In Greek art they are usually represented as riding on horseback, carrying a lance, bow, or battleaxe and a shield.

## AMBROSIA

Ambrosia, in Greek myths, was considered the food of the gods, and a substance that gave them their immortal youth. Not only did they eat of ambrosia, but they bathed in it and used it as an ointment. A god who went without ambrosia for a time suffered a loss of power, while a mortal who fed on it gained godlike strength and immortality. The adjective *ambrosial,* meaning *sweet-smelling* or *delicious,* is derived from the word.

## ANDROMACHE
Andromache was the wife of Hector of Troy, whom Homer's *Iliad* makes one of the most attractive women of antiquity. The passages describing her parting with her husband when he was setting out for his last battle, and her grief at his death, are among the most pathetic in all literature. After the fall of Troy she was taken to Greece by the son of Achilles.

## ANDROMEDA
Andromeda was a heroine of Greek mythology. Her mother, Cassiopeia, wife of the Ethiopia king Cepheus, boasted that Andromeda was more beautiful than the Nereids, and the offended sea-nymphs induced their father to send a frightful monster to ravage the coasts of Ethiopia. To secure the country from destruction Andromeda was chained to a rock to be devoured by the monster, but was rescued by Perseus. After her death she was changed to a constellation, which may be seen in the northern sky.

## ANTIGONE
Antigone, one of the most attractive characters of Greek mythology, was the constant devoted attendant of her father Oedipus. When her brother Polynices was put to death she was ordered not to bury his body, and because she disobeyed she was shut up alive in a tomb. Her story is told in the *Antigone* of Sophocles.

## APHRODITE
Aphrodite was the goddess of love and beauty (she was

called Venus by the Romans). Some legends make her the daughter of Zeus, but most of them declare that she was sprung from the foam of the sea near the island of Cythera, from where she proceeded to Cyprus, the nymphs Love and Desire attending her. When she appeared on Olympus in all her beauty, a golden wreath on her head and her silky ringlets floating about her breast, she excited the admiration of all the gods, who united to do her honor. They all proposed marriage to her, but she scornfully rejected them and provoked their enmity to such an extent that they picked out for her husband the lame and deformed Hephaestus. Aphrodite, though at first interested in Hephaestus's strange home and glowing forges, was not long faithful to such a husband, but deserted him and fell in love with Ares, Adonis, and Anchises in succession. She was a great friend of lovers, and many a time interfered to remove obstacles that separated them. Sometimes she even loaned to favored mortals her magic girdle, which had the power of inspiring love for the wearer, nor was she careful to bestow her favors justly.

APOLLO

Apollo was the radiant god of light and driver of the chariot of the sun. He was the son of Zeus and Leto, and the twin brother of Artemis, the moon-goddess, and at first was the god of light and purity merely in a physical sense. From this he came to be regarded as god of spiritual light, and so of political progress. He also presided over song and prophecy, inspiring whom he would with musical ability or with the true prophetic fervor.

In general, he was a kindly deity, smiling upon all, but stories are told of him that show that he had a sterner side. Thus when he was but five days old he killed the dreadful serpent Python, and afterward, with Artemis, put to death the children of the boasting Niobe. The Cyclopses, also, felt his vengeful spirit because they had forged the thunderbolts with which Zeus killed Aesculapius, Apollo's son.

In modern times the name Apollo is used as the symbol of manly strength and good looks, and the phrase "handsome as an Apollo" is a very common figure of speech.

## APPLE OF DISCORD

The "apple of discord" was the wonderful golden apple, in the tales of mythology, destined to be the real cause of the Trojan War. It bore the words "For the fairest of the fair," and was thrown by the goddess of discord into an assembly of the gods. Hera, Aphrodite, and Athena all claimed it, and when the Trojan Paris, chosen judge, gave it to Aphrodite, Hera became so jealous that she determined to destroy the Trojan race. Nor did she cease her plots until she had done as she planned.

## ARACHNE

According to Greek legend, Arachne was a girl so proud of her ability to weave that she dared to match her skill with that of the great goddess Athena. For her presumption Athena changed her into a spider, that she might spend her life in spinning. (The tale is told in Part IV:

Five Selected Myths.)

## ARES

Ares (called Mars by the Romans) was the god of war. His sacred emblems were the shield and spear, which the ancients believed had fallen from heaven. He personified brute strength and the wild rage of conflict. His delight was in war and bloodshed; he loved fighting for fighting's sake, and took the side of one combatant or the other indifferently, regardless of the justice of the cause. He went to battle sometimes on foot and sometimes in the war chariot made ready by his sons Deimos and Phobos (Panic and Fear), by whom he was usually accompanied.

His quarrelsomeness was regarded as inherited from his mother, Hera, and it may have been only as an illustration of the perpetual strife between his father, Zeus, and his mother that Ares was considered to be their son. According to a later tradition, he was the son of Hera alone, who became pregnant by touching a certain flower. All the gods, even Zeus, hated him, but his bitterest enemy was Athena, who knocked him to the ground with a huge stone.

In later accounts (and even in the *Odyssey*) Ares' character is somewhat toned down; thus, in the "Homeric Hymn" to Ares, he is addressed as the assistant of Themis (Justice), the enemy of tyrants, and leader of the just.

## ARETHUSA

Arethusa was a beautiful nymph, one of the attendants

of the goddess Artemis, who changed her into a fountain to free her from the too-ardent courtship of the
river god Alpheus. But the god, changing himself into a
swift torrent, still pursued her, and Artemis in pity
opened for her an underground passage through which
she fled until she came to the upper world on the plains
of Sicily. The god, however, followed her in the regions
below, and, passing from Greece to Sicily, joined his
loved one where the fountain sparkled under the bright
Sicilian skies. The Greeks based the pretty story on the
peculiar course of the Alpheus River, which, as it flows
through Arcadia toward the Ionic Sea, now and then
disappears below the surface. Near the seacoast on the
Sicilian plains a beautiful fountain bubbled up, and the
imaginative Greeks liked to believe that it contained the
waters of the Alpheus. English poet Percy Shelley wrote
the story of Arethusa in his poem of that name.

## ARGONAUTS

The Argonauts were the fabled heroes of Greece who
sailed with Jason in the *Argo* in search of the Golden
Fleece. Legend has it that long before the Trojan War,
Aenos, king of Thessaly, became tired of ruling and
gave up the throne to his brother Pelias, on condition
that the latter should rule only until Jason, the son of
Aenos, became of age. When Jason eventually demanded the crown of his uncle, Pelias pretended to
comply, but suggested that Jason and his companions
could gain great renown by going in search of the
Golden Fleece, which was known to be in the distant
land of Colchis, on the shores of the Euxine (Black) Sea.

Anxious above all things for glory, the young heroes set out on their voyage in the ship *Argo,* which had been made for them. Jason was the leader, but Orpheus, twin brothers Castor and Pollux, Hercules, and Theseus were fit companions for him. After many adventures they reached Colchis, where they learned that the Golden Fleece hung in the branches of a tree and was guarded by a dragon that never slept. Through the aid of Medea, a powerful sorceress, the daughter of the king of Colchis, a deep sleep was made to fall upon the dragon, and Jason captured the Golden Fleece and departed for Thessaly, taking Medea with him.

## ARGUS

Argus was a monster known as the *all-seeing,* because he had 100 eyes. This creature was placed by Hera to guard Io, whom she hated, but Hermes induced a deep sleep to fall upon him and then cut off his head. Hera then placed his eyes in the tail of her favorite bird, the peacock, where they may still be seen. The term "argus-eyed" is applied to one who is exceedingly watchful.

## ARIADNE

Ariadne, in Greek mythology, was a daughter of Minos, king of Crete. When Theseus came to Crete and undertook to slay the Minotaur, Ariadne gave him a twist of thread, of which she held one end. This he unwound as he entered the labyrinth, and by following it back found his way out after his victory. He fled from the island secretly, taking her with him, but deserted her on the Isle of Naxos, where she was found and married by Dionysus (Bacchus).

## ARTEMIS

In classic mythology, Artemis (called Diana by the Romans) was the daughter of Zeus and Leto, and the twin sister of Apollo. She is best known as the goddess of hunting, and is most frequently represented with bow and arrows, a quiver on her shoulder, a crescent on her head, and attended by hounds. She was brave in warfare and merciless in anger.

## ATALANTA

Atalanta was a famous Grecian huntress who declared that she would marry no man unless he could defeat her in a race. After many youths had met death for their failure, Hippomenes overcame her by stratagem and won her hand. (The tale is told in Part IV: Five Selected Myths.)

## ATHENA

Athena (also spelled Athene, but called Minerva by the Romans) was the goddess of wisdom, science, and the arts. She is represented in legend as the daughter of Zeus and Metis. Shortly before her birth her father swallowed her mother, and it came to pass that Athena sprang full-grown from the head of Zeus, clad in shining armor and singing a triumphant song of victory. Many attributes are ascribed to her by myth writers. As patroness of the arts and industries, she supervised the building of the wooden horse that caused the fall of Troy and she directed the construction of the *Argo*.

She presided over agriculture and navigation, spinning, weaving, and needlework, and though a warlike divinity, bestowed her favor only on those who practiced defensive warfare. Odysseus was her favorite warrior. It is told that Athena invented the flute, and that she cast it aside because Eros laughed at her puffed cheeks as she was playing. In the reign of Cecrops, first king of the Athenians, she contended with Poseidon for the possession of their capital city. Poseidon produced a horse as the most useful gift to mankind; Athena brought forth the olive, and to her the gods awarded the city, which was named Athens, in honor of her name. The olive tree was sacred to Athena, and oxen and cows were offered as sacrifices to her. She is sometimes represented wearing a gilt helmet and carrying a shield, and sometimes she is clad in the garb of a Grecian matron. She was the only one of the gods to whom Zeus ever entrusted his wonderful shield, the aegis.

## ATLAS

Atlas was a Titan whom Zeus condemned to bear the heavens on his shoulders. Through the centuries he stood, almost fainting with weariness, until Perseus came by, bearing the head of the Gorgon, Medusa, which turned all who looked upon it into stone. At Atlas's request, Perseus held up the head, and the giant was changed into the mountains that bear his name (located in North Africa, extending from Morocco to Tunisia). When the earliest collection of maps appeared it bore on its title page the picture of Atlas bending under the weight of the earth, and such books have therefore been called atlases to this day.

## BACCHUS (See Dionysus)

## BAUCIS AND PHILEMON
Baucis and Philemon were an aged couple who, according to the old myth, were wonderfully rewarded for their kindliness and hospitality. One evening Zeus and Hermes, who had been wandering about the earth in disguise and had been driven from a village by its unkind inhabitants, came to the cottage of Baucis and Philemon. The old couple, not recognizing their visitors, kindly received the gods and gave them the best from their frugal store. While they were at the table, Baucis and Philemon were amazed to see that the milk pitcher was no sooner emptied than it was filled again. Realizing that they were entertaining divine and not mortal guests, they fell on their knees in worship. Their little cottage was then changed into a beautiful temple, of which they were made priest and priestess, and years later, when they were very, very old, they were changed into two graceful trees, which stood beside the temple gates.

## BELLEROPHON
A mythological Greek hero, Bellerophn was the son of Glucus, king of Corinth, and the slayer of the dreadful, three-headed Chimaera. He was sent by the king of Argos to the Lycian king with a sealed message asking his death, and to accomplish this he was sent to kill the fire-breathing monster. He was assisted by the goddess Athena, who gave him the golden bridle with which he

secured the winged horse Pegasus. Mounted upon this steed, he was able to attack the monster from above and slay him.

Seeing that Bellerophon was a favorite of the gods, the king gave him his daughter in marriage and made him heir to his throne. Legend says that in his later years Bellerophon, made proud by his good fortune, attempted to mount upon Pegasus to the home of the gods, and that Zeus, angered by his boldness, caused him to be dashed to the earth. Lame and blind, he dragged out his few remaining years in misery. Nathaniel Hawthorne has told the story of Bellerophon's great victory delightfully in *The Chimaera,* omitting the later mournful part of the tale.

## BOREAS

Boreas, in Greek myths, was one of the six sons of Aeolus, god of the storms and winds, and of Eos, goddess of the dawn. Boreas personified the north wind; in classic writings he is called boisterous and blustering, and is regarded as the type of rudeness, in contrast to his youngest brother Zephyrus, the west wind, who is the type of gentleness. The origin of the term *zephyr,* applied to mild breezes, is thus explained. Aeolus sometimes sent his sons forth with orders to stir up terrible storms on the sea.

It is told by the myth writers that Boreas loved the nymph Orithyia, but that he could not woo her successfully, because it was so difficult to breathe gently and to sigh was quite out of the question. Finally, in despair, he seized her and bore her away to far-distant regions of snow and ice, where she became his wife. They were the parents of two sons and two daughters. The former, Zetes and Calais, were winged warriors who took part in the expedition of the Argonauts.

## CADMUS
Cadmus was a Greek hero who, according to legend, introduced the Phoenician alphabet into Greece. He was the son of Agenor, king of Phoenicia, and the brother of Europa. When his sister was carried off by Zeus in the form of a bull, Cadmus was directed by his father to hunt for her and not to return without her. With his brothers, he set forth on the long quest. One by one the brothers became tired and stopped by the wayside, but Cadmus kept on until told by an oracle that his search was useless. This oracle also directed him to follow a cow that he should shortly meet; and where she should lie down, there he was to found a city. He carried out these instructions, and the city that he founded was Thebes in Boeotia. After killing a dragon that guarded a fountain near the site of his proposed city, Cadmus sowed the teeth of the dragon and there sprang up a group of armed men. These men contended with one another until all but five fell, and these five became, with Cadmus, the first inhabitants of the new city.

## CALLIOPE
Calliope was one of the nine goddesses, called Muses, who presided over music, poetry and science. Calliope, whose name indicated the sweetness of her voice, was the Muse of epic poetry. In some myths she is loved by

Apollo, and their son is Orpheus, who charmed the trees and rocks and even the fierce Cerberus with his enchanting music.

CALYPSO

Calypso was a sea nymph who dwelt on a lonely island, on the shores of which Odysseus was shipwrecked. She promised Odysseus immortality if he would remain with her, and succeeded in detaining him for seven years, when he was overcome with longing to see his wife and child. At last Zeus sent the fleet Hermes to Calypso with the message that she must permit Odysseus to depart, and she helped him build the raft on which he sped upon his homeward course. She then died of grief.

CASSANDRA

Cassandra was the unhappy prophetess of Greek legend who was doomed to utter her prophecies to unbelieving ears. She was the daughter of the Trojan king and queen, Priam and Hecuba, and was loved by Apollo, from whom she received the power to foretell the future. When she would not return his love the angry god decreed that none should believe her words. Again and again she warned her countrymen not to keep the stolen wife of Menelaus, the beautiful Helen, and she vainly begged them not to take the Wooden Horse within the walls of Troy. In some of the Grecian myths she is carried away to Greece by Agamemnon and there murdered by his wife, Clytemnestra. This story is told by Aeschylus in his tragedy *Agamemnon*.

## CASTOR AND POLLUX

Castor and Pollux were the twin sons of Zeus and Leda, and the heroes of some of the most picturesque stories in Greek mythology. They are often called the *Dioscuri,* which means *sons of Zeus.* The "illustrious twins," as Horace speaks of them, were champions of the manly sports, Castor favoring especially the art of horsemanship and Pollux that of boxing. Helen of Troy was their sister. One of their exploits was their invasion of Attica to rescue her from Theseus, who had carried her off to Athens. They also shared in the dangers of the Calydonian hunt, in which the greatest heroes of Greece engaged in order to rid the fields of Calydon of a ravenous boar. They sailed on the Argonautic expedition and were afterwards honored as patrons of voyagers.

Castor, who was mortal, was slain in battle, and Zeus, to comfort the grieving Pollux, permitted him to share his immortality with his brother. Thus the brothers lived one day in Olympus, and the next in Hades. According to another story, Zeus placed them among the stars as Gemini, the Twins.

## CECROPS

Cecrops was a character who figures in Greek tradition as the first king of Attica and the builder of the famous citadel of Athens, named Cecropia in his honor. Various stories sprang up about him; he was said to have introduced marriage, the burial of the dead, and writing and other arts. In the myths he is a half snake, half man, who came from Crete or from Egypt and founded the city of Athens. When Athena and Poseidon disputed as to which should have the honor of naming the city, Cecrops decided in favor of Athena.

## CENTAUR

A centaur was a mythical creature, half man, half horse, supposed by the ancient Greeks to live in Thessaly. Although wild and lawless, the centaurs were represented as capable of good attributes, for the centaur Chiron was one of the wisest teachers of the great Greek heroes. At one time, when a certain king was being married, the centaurs appeared at the celebration and tried to carry off the bride. The battle that ensued was one of the favorite subjects in Greek art. An interesting explanation of the centaur myth is that the early Greeks, totally unacquainted with horseback riding, saw occasional riders come out of Thessaly and fancied that man and horse were one being.

## CERBERUS

In Greek myths, Cerberus was Hades' three-headed dog, the grim guardian of the entrance to the underworld. His jaws dripped with foam, from which sprang the deadly nightshade (a plant with poisonous berries). Early and late he kept his watch, allowing no living being to enter the gates of Hades, nor any spirit to pass out of them. Orpheus, however, searching for his wife Eurydice, played such melting strains on his lyre that Cerberus was won over and permitted him, though a mortal, to enter the realms of Hades.

The last of Hercules' twelve labors was the descent into Hades to secure the savage Cerberus. Hercules speedily accomplished this fearful task, but when he brought the triple-headed monster to Eurystheus, at whose command the deed was performed, the latter fled in terror, and taking refuge in a huge jar would not come out of his hiding place until Hercules had carried the dog back to Hades.

## CHARON

Charon was the ragged old ferryman of the Lower World. He is represented as the son of Erebus and Nyx, bent and old, with matted beard and tattered garments. Gloomily, with one oar, he ferried the shades of the dead across the rivers Styx and Acheron to the realm of Hades. But the mythological story tells us that he would take only those who had had a proper burial, and in whose mouths was placed an *obolus,* the coin Charon exacted as his fee. All others were compelled to wander wearily on the shores of the river for a century; after that time Charon would take them without charge to their final resting place.

Charon appears frequently in literature and art. Homer does not mention him, but he is pictured in Vergil's *Aeneid.* The hero Aeneas is ferried across to Hades in the boat that had previously carried only spirits of the dead. Though Charon for a long time refused to perform this service, he was finally persuaded to do it. On some early Etruscan monuments he appears as an ugly, animal-faced demon of death, with tusks and pointed ears, carrying snakes or a large hammer.

CHARYBDIS (See Scylla and Charybdis)

## CHIMAERA

The Chimaera, in the stories of Homer, was a fire-breathing female monster with the head of a lion, the body of a goat, and the tail of a serpent, that long laid waste the land of Lycia and Caria. The hero Bellerophon, commissioned by the Lycian king, Iobates, to destroy this creature, procured with the help of Athena the winged steed Pegasus, and speeding through the air, found the Chimaera and killed her.

The word *chimerical,* derived from *Chimaera,* has come to be applied to any idea or plan that is wild or fantastic.

## CHIRON

Chiron, in Greek mythology, was the famous learned centaur (half horse, half man) who taught such renowned heroes as Achilles, Hercules, Odysseus and Aeneas. Chiron was the son of Cronos and Philyra, and became skilled in medicine, music, hunting, and the art of prophecy, under the instruction of Apollo and Artemis. He lived at the foot of Mount Pelion, in Thessaly. One day the other centaurs were driven into Chiron's home by Hercules, and by accident a poisoned arrow from the bow of his old pupil struck Chiron. The poison caused him such torture that Zeus mercifully ended Chiron's life on earth and placed him among the stars, where he became the constellation Sagittarius, or the Archer.

## CIRCE

In Greek legend Circe was a beautiful sorceress, said to have been the daughter of Helios and the sea nymph Perse. For the murder of her husband she had been banished to the island of Aeaea, on the coast of Italy. To there she lured unfortunate travelers, and by means of drugs and enchantments changed them to animals. While Odysseus and his companions were seeking their way home to Ithaca after the fall of Troy, they came to the island of Circe, where all the companions fell under the spell and were changed to swine. Odysseus himself escaped by using the herb given him by Hermes, and he compelled Circe to restore his companions to human form. The best-known story of Circe is to be found in the *Odyssey* of Homer.

## CLYTEMNESTRA

Clytemnestra, in Greek mythology, was the unfaithful and treacherous wife of Agamemnon and half-sister of Helen, Castor, and Pollux. The poet Homer tells how, during the absence of her husband in the war against Troy, she bestowed her favors on Aegisthus. On Agamemnon's return they murdered him to hide their guilt, and together governed Mycenae for years. Her son Orestes later avenged his father's death by killing both Clytemnestra and her lover.

## CRONUS

Cronus (also spelled Chronos and Kronos, but called Saturn by the Romans) was the youngest of the Titans and son of Uranus (Heaven) and Gaea (Earth). He overthrew his father and became ruler of the universe and was happy until the birth of his first child. Then he remembered that an oracle had declared that he should be dethroned by his child, and to prevent this he swallowed the babe. Four other children met a like fate, but when Zeus, the sixth and last, was born, the mother concealed the babe and gave Cronus in its stead a stone, wrapped in child's clothing, which he swallowed without noticing the substitution. When Zeus grew up he dethroned his father and banished him to Italy, where he set up a most prosperous kingdom. He taught the people agriculture and useful arts, and his reign in Italy was known as the Golden Age. Cronus is shown in art as an old man bent with infirmities. In his hand he holds a scythe and a serpent, which bites its own tail—emblems of time and of the year. Cronus himself is the personification of time, and the story of his swallowing his children is but an allegorical way of saying that time creates only to destroy.

CYCLOPS

In Grecian legend, a Cyclops was a member of a race of giant shepherds. Each had only one eye, which was placed in the middle of the forehead. These giants dwelt in Sicily. In the story of Hesiod they were the sons of Uranus and Gaea, or Heaven and Earth, and were slain by Apollo for having furnished Zeus with thunderbolts to kill Asclepius. In the *Odyssey,* Odysseus escaped death by blinding the Cyclops Polyphemus.

## DAEDALUS

Daedalus was a sculptor, architect, and artisan of Greek mythology, worshiped by ancient artists' guilds as the personification of art and as the inventor of carpentry and many tools. The name is from the Greek, and means *the cunning worker*. Through jealousy, according to the myth, Daedalus killed his nephew and pupil, Talos, and was obliged to flee from Athens to Crete. There he built Ariadne's dancing grounds and the famous labyrinth that confined the Minotaur. Later, having offended the king, he and his son, Icarus, were imprisoned. To achieve an escape, Daedalus made two pairs of wings, which they fastened on their shoulders. According to the myth, Icarus fell into the sea, because he flew so near the sun that the wax that fastened the wings was melted. Daedalus landed safely in Sicily, where he built several famous temples.

## DAPHNE

In classic myths, Daphne was a beautiful nymph who delighted in woodland sports and hunting, the daughter of the river-god Peneus. She desired to remain unmarried, like Artemis, but her beauty brought many lovers. Apollo, especially, pierced by a golden arrow from Eros's bow, was filled with love for her. But Daphne, pierced by Eros's leaden arrow, abhorred the thought of loving. One day Apollo chased Daphne through the woods, and when her strength failed she called on her father to change her form. Immediately she was changed into a laurel tree, and ever after the laurel was sacred to Apollo. He wore a wreath of its leaves as a crown and since then laurel wreaths have been symbols of honor and merit.

## DEMETER

Demeter (called Ceres by the Romans) was a goddess who protected and watched over the fruits of the earth, and especially the grains. She was the daughter of Cronus and Rhea and mother of Persephone. According to the interesting myth, when her daughter was stolen and carried off to Hades, Demeter neglected the earth during her search for Persephone, and all vegetation died. Demeter was usually represented in full attire, holding ears of corn and a lighted torch, and with poppies, her sacred flower.

## DEUCALION

Deucalion, the Noah of Greek mythology, was the mythological son of Prometheus. He and his wife Pyrrha, as faithful servants of the gods, were the only ones saved when Zeus caused a deluge to destroy the world on account of the wickedness of mankind. In a wooden chest made on the advice of Prometheus, Deucalion and Pyrrha floated on the waters nine days, finally landing on the summit of Mount Parnassus. When the deluge subsided, finding the land depopulated, they sought the oracle at Delphi for information as to how they could repopulate the earth. They were told to throw behind them the bones of their mother. Interpreting that to mean their mother earth, they threw stones over their shoulders, which on striking the earth became men and women, strong and hardy. Deucalion became the ancestor of the Greeks through his son Hellen.

## DIONYSUS

Dionysus (also known as Bacchus), the god of wine, was the son of Zeus and Semele. In early times he was connected with the springing up of plant life, and he taught how to cultivate the vine and how to make the wine from the fruit. Great feasts, known as *Bacchanalia,* or *Dionysia,* were held at Athens in his honor. In art the forehead of the god is crowned with vine leaves or ivy, and he is represented as naked, or wearing a wide mantle about his shoulders and a fawn skin across his breast.

The worshipers of Dionysus (Bacchus), both men and women, were called *Bacchantes.* These people, at the time of the feast of Bacchus, would gather on the woody heights, and, roused to frenzy by wine and excitement, would spend days and nights in dancing and rioting. In modern speech, *bacchanalian* is applied to riotous or drunken revels.

## DRYADS

In classical mythology, dryads (or hamadryads) were the wood nymphs who danced with the god Pan. It was believed that with each tree a dryad came into existence and that she, too, perished when the tree died. Purposely to destroy a tree, the house of a dryad, was considered an impious act and was punished accordingly. These graceful nymphs of the woodlands at times assumed the forms of followers of the hunt, peasant girls or shepherdesses.

## ECHO

In Greek mythology, Echo was a beautiful nymph, an attendant of Artemis, the huntress, and noted for her conversational powers. On one occasion when the jealous Hera was seeking her husband Zeus, believing him to be with the nymphs, Echo detained her in conversation until Zeus escaped. The goddess punished her by condemning her never to speak first, and always to repeat the last word she heard from others. A more poetic version is that Echo fell in love with Narcissus, a beautiful youth insensible to love, and because he did not return her affection she pined away until nothing was left but her voice, which may still be heard in the mountains, speaking only when spoken to and replying only in the exact words of the speaker. Many poets have found inspiration in this legend, among them Shelley in his poem "Adonais."

## ELYSIUM

In classical mythology, Elysium (also known as the Elysian Fields) was the home of the good and blessed after death. When a soul left this world it was tried before three judges of Hades, the god of the dead. If the good outweighed the evil, the soul was sent to this beautiful region, which had sun, moon, and stars of its own and where all were happy and joyful. Early writers, such as Homer, considered the "Isles of the Blessed" as Elysium, while in later times it was thought to be a section of the lower world.

## ENDYMION

Endymion, in Greek mythology, was a beautiful youth who had asked Zeus for eternal slumber, and whom, while he was sleeping on Mount Latmos, Artemis saw and kissed. The legends regarding him vary greatly, describing him as a king, a hunter, and a shepherd. The myth was the inspiration for English poet John Keats' "Endymion."

## EOS

Eos (called Aurora by the Romans) was the goddess of the dawn, the radiant messenger who opened the gates of the East, so that the sun god in his chariot might drive up the sky. Her rosy fingers and yellow robe represented the glowing colors that appear in the heavens before the sun rises. Eos was a somewhat fickle goddess, and bestowed her love in turn upon Orion, Tithonus, and Cephalus.

## EREBUS

Erebus, the primeval god of darkness, was one of the sons of Chaos. The name is used especially to denote the dark and gloomy cavern beneath the earth to which no gleam of sunshine ever penetrated and through which the spirits of the dead passed on the way to Hades. It was over this mysterious world that Erebus reigned. Nyx, his sister, represented Night, and was worshiped by the ancients with the greatest solemnity.

## ERIS

Eris, in classic mythology, was the goddess of discord

and the sister of the war-god Ares. In the legend of the Trojan War, Eris is the goddess who, indignant that she was the only one of all the gods and goddesses who was not invited to the marriage festivities of Peleus and Thetis, threw into the midst of the guests a golden apple—known ever since as the "apple of discord"—which bore the inscription, "For the fairest of the fair." This sparked a rivalry between the three deities—Hera, Athena, and Aphrodite—for the gift was left to the judgment of Paris, the son of the king of Troy, who, being appointed umpire by Zeus, bestowed it on Aphrodite.

In the *Iliad,* Eris, or Strife, is described at first as insignificant, but as swelling until her head touches the heavens. In the *Aeneid* she appears under the name of Discordia.

### EROS

Eros (called Cupid by the Romans) was the god of love of classic mythology, represented in sculpture and painting as a beautiful, chubby, naked boy with gauzy wings and a roguish, dimpled face, and armed with a bow and a quiver of arrows. No other character of mythology has been adopted more generally into the literature and sentiment of the present day. This "archer of archers" is usually spoken of as blind or blindfolded.

Eros was the son of Ares, god of war, and of Aphrodite, the goddess of love. The legend is that he loved a mortal princess named Psyche, who after many trials was made immortal by the gods. As Eros is the emblem of the heart, Psyche is the symbol of the soul. Long ago

Eros was at times represented with a helmet, a spear, and a small shield, and riding on the back of a lion or on a dolphin, to show his power.

## EUROPA

According to Greek legend, Europa was a daughter of Phoenix, king of Phoenicia, or of Agenor, and the sister of Cadmus. She was admired by Zeus, who appeared in the form of a white bull, and carried her to Crete, where she bore him three sons (Minos, Rhadamanthus, and Sarpedon). The bull, whose form Zeus assumed, is the same bull we recognize in the constellation Taurus. Contrary to belief sometimes expressed, the word *Europe* is not derived from this name.

## EURYDICE

Eurydice, in Greek mythology, was the wife of Orpheus. After her death from the bite of a serpent, her husband descended into Hades and so charmed Hades with the music of his lyre that he was permitted to take Eurydice back to earth, on condition, however, that he should precede her on the way to the upper regions and that he should not look behind him. Orpheus, yielding to his natural anxiety, disobeyed this latter injunction, and Eurydice was drawn back into the infernal regions. There is no possible connection between this story and the Bible narrative of Lot's wife, although there is a popular belief to that effect. The tales simply happen to run parallel, so far as is known. A beautiful version of the legend is found in Vergil's *Georgics*.

## EUTERPE

Euterpe was one of the nine Muses in classical mythology, created by Zeus in answer to a request on the part of the victorious deities, after the war with the Titans, that some special divinities be called into existence to commemorate in song the glorious deeds of the Olympian gods. Euterpe, whose name means *she who delights,* was the Muse of lyric poetry. She is represented as a virgin crowned with flowers and holding an instrument in her hand, usually a flute. The invention of the flute was attributed to her.

## FATES

The Fates were three goddesses who were supposed by the Greeks to preside over human destinies and spin the thread of life. Originally the three were said to exercise their powers collectively, but later legends divided them, allotting certain tasks to each. *Clotho,* the spinner, spun the thread of life; *Lachesis* traced the fate of man; *Atropos* cut the thread of life with the shears of destiny. In ancient art *Clotho* was usually distinguished by a spindle, *Lachesis* by rods held in her hand, from which she drew the lot of man; *Atropos* held in her hand a roll or tablet on which she recorded the fate, or depicted by pointing to a sundial the hour at which man must meet his death. The Fates were gloomy, unsympathetic goddesses, inflexible in purpose, worshiped and propitiated as beings who punished man but never conferred blessings.

## FURIES

The Furies, in Greek mythology, were three sisters

named Alecto, Tisiphone, and Megaera, who were attendants of Persephone, the goddess of death and the underworld. They sprang from the blood of the wounded Uranus, and were noted for their hard hearts as well as the merciless manner in which they hurried the ghosts entrusted to their care over the fiery flood of the river Phlegethon to eternal torment. Their heads were wreathed with serpents and they watched remorselessly for every soul they could catch.

## GAEA
In Greek mythology, Gaea, a goddess, was the personification of the earth. She was the first-born of Chaos (the personification of infinite, empty space, which existed before all things) and the mother of Uranus and Pontus. By Uranus she was the mother of Oceanus, Cronus, and many others. Homer makes her the mother of Erechtheus and Tithyus.

## GALATEA
Galatea, a sea nymph of classic mythology, was the daughter of Nereus and Doris and has often been called the *queen of the sea*. Ugly, one-eyed Polyphemus loved her, but she gave herself to the Sicilian shepherd Acis. Enraged at this, the monster, surprising them one day, crushed Acis beneath a rock, so turning him into a stream, which flowed to the sea to meet the beloved Galatea. (For the story of the statue of Galatea, see Pygmalion.)

## GANYMEDE

Ganymede was a youth of marvelous beauty whom Zeus, in the form of an eagle, kidnapped and carried off to Olympus to be his cupbearer (server of nectar). Hebe, the goddess of youth, had always poured the nectar in which the gods often pledged themselves, until one day at a solemn occasion she tripped and fell. This accident disgraced her and she was forced to resign her office. So Zeus, in the form of an eagle, left Olympus in search of her successor, and flew over the earth until he saw this beautiful youth, the son of the king of Troy. Swooping down, he caught the boy in his mighty talons and carried him back to the top of his mountain, where he was taught his duties as cupbearer to the gods.

## GOLDEN FLEECE

In Greek mythology the Golden Fleece was a fleece (wooly covering of a sheep) of gold that was guarded by a dragon in a grove sacred to Ares, in the city of Colchis, on the shore of the Black Sea. That Jason might prove himself worthy of the throne of Iolcus, which he claimed from the usurper Pelias, his uncle, he was commissioned to bring back the Golden Fleece. He started on this perilous adventure with a band of heroes, who sailed in the ship *Argo*. Many were the thrilling experiences that the Argonauts encountered, but Jason secured the Fleece and returned to Iolcus to demand the abdication of the wicked Pelias.

## GORGONS

The Gorgons were three frightful sisters of Greek mythology who had the power to turn anyone who looked at them to stone. The two older ones, Stheno and Euryale, were immortal, but Medusa, the one best known, was mortal and met her death at the hands of Perseus. The hair of the Gorgons was a mass of serpents, their hands and teeth were of brass, and their bodies were covered with scales that could not be pierced. The name is from a Greek word meaning *grim,* and is often used to signify anything very hideous.

GRACES

In Greek mythology the Three Graces, the daughters of Zeus and Eurynome, were the three goddesses who presided over the dance, the banquet, and all kindred pleasures and polite accomplishments. They are three sisters, and as such always inseparable. They are in essence the soul in its fullness of life and sympathy, pouring itself rhythmically through every obstruction, before which the most solid becomes fluid, transparent, and radiant of itself. In the writings of the Greek poet Hesiod they are given the names of Aglaia (Brightness), Euphrosyne (Joy), and Thalia (Bloom). Homer represents them in the *Odyssey* as the attendants of Aphrodite. In art they are grouped together, usually embracing each other or clasping hands.

HADES

In Greek mythology, both the underworld itself (the abode of the spirits of the dead, unvisited by a single ray of the sun) and the god of that underworld are known as Hades. The god Hades (called Pluto by the Romans), son of Cronus and Rhea, brother of Zeus and Poseidon, left his realm but once, and then in search of Persephone, whom he made his queen.

## HARPIES

In Greek mythology the harpies were the ministers of divine vengeance, defiling everything they touched. A harpy was represented as a winged monster, having the face and body of a woman, the wings of a bird of prey, and with feet and fingers armed with sharp claws. The harpies were generally supposed to be two or three in number, but occasionally several others were mentioned; Homer refers to but one. Originally they were conceived to be storm winds, but were later represented as winged maidens, their general characteristics being hideously repulsive.

## HEBE

In ancient myth Hebe was the goddess of youth, who poured out the nectar with which the gods pledged each other. One day, upon a solemn occasion, she tripped and fell. Then she was forced to resign her office, while her father, Zeus, went in search of another cupbearer, finally kidnapping the beautiful youth Ganymede for the office. Hebe always retained the power of restoring the aged to the bloom of youth and beauty, and some accounts say that it was only after she became the wife of Hercules, who was deified, that she gave up her office of cupbearer. She even succeeded in reconciling her mother, Hera, to Hercules, who had suffered all his life from the hatred of the queen of the gods.

## HECATE

Hecate was a mythological goddess of dark places who is often associated with ghosts and sorcery. She is frequently represented as having three heads, or three bodies, with serpents around her neck and shoulders. She had the power to bestow or withhold at pleasure the blessing of wealth, victory, wisdom, and good luck to mortals, and was the only goddess who retained power under the rule of Zeus. She was subsequently confounded with several other divinities, such as Demeter, Artemis, and Persephone, and at last became a mystic goddess, having all the powers of Nature. Magicians and witches claimed her as their infernal goddess. Offerings of dogs, honey, and eggs were made to her at places where three roads met.

## HECTOR

In Greek mythology Hector was the most valiant of the Trojans, whose forces he commanded. He engaged the Grecian heroes in conflicts and often gained advantage over them. By his presence Troy was unconquerable, but when he killed Patroclus, the friend of Achilles, the latter slew him and dragged his body about the walls of the city at his chariot wheels. Priam, the father of Hector, afterward got possession of the body and gave it solemn burial. In the sixth book of the *Iliad,* Hector's leave-taking of his wife, Andromache, and his departure to meet Achilles for the last time are the finest episodes described therein.

## HECUBA

In Greek mythology Hecuba was the second wife of
Priam, king of Troy, and, according to Homer, mother
of nineteen of Priam's fifty sons, including Hector,
Paris, and Troilus. In the overthrow of Troy, Priam was
slain, and Hecuba was given as a slave to Odysseus. According to one form of the legend, Hecuba, in despair,
leaped into the Hellespont (a strait between Greece and
Turkey).

## HELEN OF TROY

Helen of Troy was the fairest woman of the ancient
world, whose name to every age since her own time has
stood for all that is most beautiful. According to popular myth, she was the daughter of Zeus and Leda, whom
the king of all the gods had courted in the semblance of
a swan. When but a child she was so beautiful that Theseus bore her off to be his bride, but she was brought
back to her Spartan home, and as she grew she in-
creased in beauty so that thirty ardent suitors sought her
hand. Proclaiming Menelaus, king of Sparta, as her
choice, she bound the other suitors by an oath that they
would help her husband in his need. When Paris, son of
Priam, king of Troy, became a guest in Menelaus' home,
he pleaded with Helen that she go with him back to his
father's house, and he won his suit. Some of the legends
declare she went willingly, while others assume that
Paris carried her to Troy by force. Forsaken Menelaus
called on all those Grecian chiefs whose sacred oath he
held, and they came forward to avenge his wrong. This
was the cause of the great Trojan War, the most terrific

conflict of old times.

When Troy had fallen, Helen, whose beauty still could drive men to despair, returned to Menelaus, whom she found ready to take her once more as his wife. Their later life in Sparta, their old home, passed happily for them, but all her days were saddened by the thoughts of all the woe that Greece had suffered for her beauty's sake.

## HELIOS

In Greek legend Helios was the sun god, child of the Titan Hyperion and the Titaness Theia, and brother of Eos. He was later identified with Apollo. According to the myth, he dwelt in a magnificent palace in the east, which he left in the morning to pursue his light-giving labors and to which he was conveyed at night in a winged boat of gold. He was widely worshiped, and had temples in Corinth, Argos, Elis, and elsewhere, with headquarters at Rhodes. In art he was represented as a beautiful youth with hair unbound and crowned by rays.

## HELLESPONT

Hellespont is the ancient name of the narrow channel that connects the Sea of Marmora with the Aegean Sea and now called the *Dardanelles*. It was named after Helle, daughter of the king of Boeotia, who fell from the back of the ram with the Golden Fleece during her flight from the wrath of Ino, and was drowned in the channel. In legend and poetry the Hellespont is famed as the channel across which Leander swam nightly to visit the priestess Hero, and in which he lost his life when the light in her tower failed to guide him.

## HEPHAESTUS

Hephaestus (called Vulcan by the Romans) was the god of fire and the patron of the blacksmith and the artist in metal. He was the son of Zeus and Hera, or, as one fable says, of Hera alone, who produced him that she might not be eclipsed by Zeus, who had given birth to Athena. Hephaestus was born lame and more or less deformed, and so shocked was his mother that she threw him from Olympus; but he was saved and brought up by the nymphs and Nereids, in a cave beneath the ocean, where he gained his marvelous skill in the fashioning of objects from metal.

It is said that in one of the quarrels between Zeus and Hera, the latter was suspended between heaven and earth with anvils hanging to her person. Hephaestus saw her there and attempted to rescue her, but was detected in the attempt. This so incensed Zeus that he kicked the young god out of heaven and in the terrible fall that ensued, Hephaestus was still further crushed and maimed. He never returned to Olympus to live, though often he was called to build great palaces for the other gods and always he forged the thunderbolts of Zeus. He was exceedingly skillful in the use of metals and many of the objects that he made he was able to endow with life. He made brass-throated, fire-breathing bulls, gold and silver dogs that guarded the houses of his friends, and for himself he fashioned golden maidens, endowed with reason and speech, who waited upon him at his home. His wife, according to some accounts, was Charis, but it is also said that he was married for a time to Aphrodite, who, however, grew weary of him.

This god is usually represented as a serene old man with muscular form, whose hair hangs in curls on his shoulders.

## HERA

Hera (called Juno by the Romans) was the chief goddess of classical mythology. She was regarded as queen of the gods and of heaven, and was also the especial genius of the female sex, worshiped by women as the protectress of all that concerned marriage and the birth of children. She was represented as the jealous and exacting wife of Zeus, and her life was not a very happy one. She spent a great deal of time in planning punishments for Zeus's mortal wives or their sons. She was supposed to be a very beautiful, matronly woman. In works of art Hera is sometimes represented as drawn through the air by a pair of sacred peacocks harnessed to her chariot. The goose and the cuckoo were also sacred to her.

## HERCULES

Hercules (also known as Heracles) was the great national hero of the ancient Greeks, famed for his incomparable strength and mighty deeds of valor and endurance. In the myths of Hercules the ancients gave expression to their worship of all that was manly and heroic. The great mythical hero was said to be the son of Zeus, the greatest of the gods, and Alcmene, a princess of mortal origin. When the tidings of his birth were conveyed to Hera, queen of the gods, she determined that the child of her rival should perish, and forthwith sent two gigantic serpents to the palace where he was lying in his cradle. Just as they were about to crush him in their folds, the baby Hercules caught them by the neck and strangled them.

The education of the boy was supervised by Chiron, a famous centaur, who taught him the use of all weapons and gave him training in the various athletic sports. When his education was completed, he went forth into the world, and in the course of time was happily married to Megara, daughter of Creon, king of Thebes. While he was enjoying a peaceful and prosperous life, Hera, still his bitter enemy, caused him to be seized with madness, and in this condition he killed his wife and three children. When he regained his reason he suffered untold agony and remorse for his terrible deed, to atone for which he offered his services to his cousin Eurystheus, king of Argus. Twelve mighty labors were imposed by his royal master as deeds of atonement, as follows:

1. The first labor was the destruction of a bloodthirsty lion that had made its lair in the Nemean Forest. Boldly entering the den of the monster, Hercules grasped it by the throat and strangled it to death, after which he made for himself a coat of its shaggy skin.

2. For his second task he slew the Hydra, a seven-headed serpent that was ravaging the Areshes of Lerna.

3. The third labor imposed by Eurystheus was the capture of the golden-horned stag of Cerynea, whose brazen feet carried him along so swiftly they seemed scarcely to touch the ground. Hercules overtook this

fleet animal after a long, weary chase, but succeeded in capturing him only by driving him into a far northern snowdrift from which he could not make his escape.

4. The capture of the wild boar of Erymanthus, in Arcadia, was his fourth desperate adventure. In the midst of this labor he was attacked by the centaurs, whom he vanquished by turning upon them his death-bringing arrows.

5. Hercules was next commanded to cleanse the stables of Augeas (king of Elis), which contained over a thousand cattle and which had not been cleaned in over thirty years. To accomplish this he rerouted the rushing torrent of the River Alpheus to clean out the filth.

6. For his sixth task he was sent forth to slay the brazen-clawed birds that hovered over the waters of Lake Stymphalus, and that ate human flesh. With his poisoned arrows he destroyed the entire flock of these savage birds.

7. His seventh labor was the capture of a mad bull given by Poseidon to Minos, king of Crete, which in its frenzy was laying waste the entire island.

8. He next journeyed to Thrace, whose king, Diomedes, owned a number of beautiful horses that fed on human flesh. As his eighth labor Hercules delivered these fearful steeds to Eurystheus.

9. On his ninth adventure he visited the country of the Amazons to obtain for the daughter of Eurystheus the girdle worn by the Amazon queen, Hippolyta. This prize he bore away only after he had fought and defeated the warlike race of women, who were misled by Hera into believing that the hero had come to kidnap

their queen.

10. His tenth task was the capture of the oxen of Geryon, a creature with three bodies who made his home in the island of Erythea. This island lay far to the west, bathed in the light of the setting sun, and to reach it Hercules had to pass through many different countries. When he came to the frontiers of Libya and Europe, he raised as memorials of his journey the two mountains of Abyla and Calpe, the famous Pillars of Hercules. On reaching Erythea, he slew the guards of the oxen, the giant Eurytion and his two-headed dog, and bore his trophies back in triumph to Eurystheus.

11. Even more difficult than this was the eleventh labor, the seizure of the golden apples of the Hesperides (a group of sisters who, with the aid of a dragon, guarded the golden apples). To secure these he asked for the help of Atlas, father of the Hesperides, who bore the heavens on this shoulders. Hercules himself bore on his shoulders the mighty burden while Atlas plucked the glittering fruit from the gardens.

12. His final task was the most difficult of all, the descent into the realm of Hades, the god of the lower world, to bring up the dog Cerberus, grim guardian of Hades. When he laid the ferocious monster at the feet of Eurystheus, that king fled in terror and hid himself in a huge jar.

When all his labors were completed the hero wandered forth to enjoy the happiness of long-desired freedom. Too soon, however, was he forced to return to bondage, for, having slain his friend Iphitus in a fit of anger, he was condemned to serve Omphale, queen of

Lydia, for a period of three years. Omphale clad herself in his lion's skin and made her hero-slave dress in a woman's garb, while with awkward hands he worked at spinning.

After he had been released from the Lydian queen, he married Deianira, who accompanied him in his wanderings. One day they came to a rapidly flowing stream, across which Deianira was carried by the centaur Nessus. The centaur, on reaching the opposite shore, started to run away with his fair burden, and Hercules, hearing her cries, shot her captor with one of his poisoned arrows. Nessus, with his dying breath, told Deianira to dip in his blood a robe of Hercules, which he said would bring back her husband's love if ever it wandered from her.

When, some time later, she became jealous of Iole, a captive maiden, she unwittingly sent to Hercules the robe, poisoned with the blood of Nessus. The hero at once put it on, and as the poison penetrated his body, in a frenzy of pain he tried to wrench away the garment, but only tore off great pieces of his own flesh.

In his agony he uprooted great pines, and Lichas, who had brought the robe to him, he flung into the sea from the heights of Mount Oeta. Finally, to end the unbearable pain, he erected a huge funeral pile on the mountain, laid himself upon it, and commanded his friend Philoctetes to apply the torch. When the flames had consumed all of him that was mortal, great Zeus descended from heaven and bore away his soul to the abode of the gods, where, wedded to the goddess Hebe, he lived in everlasting happiness.

## HERMES

Hermes (called Mercury by the Romans) was an important deity in classical mythology who served as the messenger of the gods, and particularly of Zeus, whose son he was. He presided over eloquence and was the patron of orators and merchants, and also of dishonest persons, thieves, and robbers; besides, he ruled over roads and conducted the souls of the dead to Hades. From his birth he was most remarkable, for before noon of the first day of his life he had invented the lyre, and by evening had stolen the cattle of Admetus, which Apollo was tending, and had hidden them. Forced to admit his guilt and to restore the cattle, he confessed that he had eaten ten of them, and in payment he offered Apollo his lyre. The sun god was so pleased with the gift that he gave Hermes in exchange the *caduceus* (herald's wand, with two serpents twined around it).

Hermes was a great favorite with the gods because of his pranks as well as of his wit and intelligence. Zeus gave him a winged cap and winged sandals and a short, scythe-like sword, and by means of these he performed many wonders as the spy and servant of the king of gods. It was he who fixed Ixion to his revolving wheel, who slew the giant Argus, conducted Priam to the tent of Achilles, carried Dionysus to the nymphs, sold Hercules to Omphale, and brought Persephone back from the underworld. In art Hermes is often shown with his winged cap, winged sandals, and caduceus.

## HERO

Hero, in mythology, was the beautiful priestess who

placed a bright light at the top of her lonely tower each night to guide her lover, Leander, as he swam across the Hellespont to see her. No one suspected their meetings, and all went well until the first severe storms of winter swept over the sea. Then one morning, after watching all night in the storm, Hero found the body of her lover tossing on the waves at the foot of her tower. In despair she threw herself into the sea and perished at his side.

### HESPERIDES

In Greek legend the Heperides were four sisters, Agle, Arethusa, Erytheia, and Hesperia, the daughters of Atlas and Hesperis, who guarded the golden apples that Gaea, or Earth, presented to Hera on her marriage to Zeus. The sleepless dragon, Ladon, assisted the maidens in their guardianship of the sacred fruit. It was the eleventh labor of Hercules to obtain the golden apples.

### HESTIA

Hestia (called Vesta by the Romans), daughter of Cronus and Rhea, was the Greek goddess of the hearth, or rather the fire that burns in it; the guardian of domestic life, the personification of the idea of home. When Apollo and Poseidon became suitors for her hand, she swore to remain a maiden forever, whereupon Zeus bestowed upon her the honor of presiding over all sacrifices. The fire of Hestia was always kept burning, and, if by any accident it became extinct, only sacred fire produced by friction, or by burning glasses drawing fire from the sun, might be used to rekindle it.

## HYDRA

In Greek legend Hydra was a monster that dwelt in Lake Lerna, in Argolis. It was credited with possessing many heads, of which the central one was immortal. The number of heads varied from nine to a hundred, any one of which being cut off was immediately replaced by two others, unless the wound was seared by fire. The destruction of this monster was the second labor of Hercules, and was accomplished with the assistance of Iolaus who, as each head was cut off, cauterized the wound. The immortal head was buried beneath a huge stone.

## HYGEIA

In Greek mythology Hygeia was the goddess of health and the daughter of Aesculapius, with whom she was worshiped at Athens, Corinth, and elsewhere. She is represented in art accompanied by her father, or sometimes alone, with a snake at her side, the symbol of healing power delegated to her from Apollo. Originally, Hygeia was an independent goddess, but later was joined with other deities who were identified with the cure of disease. The origin of the modern word hygiene is thus accounted for.

## HYMEN

Hymen was originally the name of a marriage song among the Greeks, but later applied by them to the god of marriage, whose blessing was invoked at every wedding. He was generally regarded as a son of Apollo and a Muse, but sometimes of Dionysus and Aphrodite. In art he is represented as a youth of delicate beauty, wearing a crown of flowers and carrying a torch.

## HYPERION

In the oldest legends of Greece, Hyperion was one of the twelve children of Uranus and Gaea, who constituted a race of giants known as the Titans. Uranus, fearing the power of his gigantic offspring, shut them up in the lower regions, but Gaea loosed the bonds of Cronus, the most daring of the twelve. He then set free his brothers and sisters and to each gave a portion of the world to govern. To Hyperion was assigned the direction of the sun, which he drove across the sky each day in a golden chariot. In later mythology Hyperion was identified with Apollo, god of the sun.

## IO

In Greek mythology Io was the daughter of the king of Argos. She was beloved by Zeus, who, to protect her from the jealousy of Hera, changed her into a white heifer (a young cow that has not borne a calf). Hera contrived, however, to obtain the animal from Zeus, and gave her to the care of the hundred-eyed Argus, from whom she was rescued by Hermes. Hera then sent a gadfly (a fly that bites livestock) to torment the unfortunate Io, and the latter wandered all over the world in her attempts to escape from her tormentor. In Egypt she found rest and freedom from persecution. On the banks of the Nile she assumed her original form. Her son Epaphus, later king of Egypt, was the reputed founder of the famous ancient Egyptian city of Memphis.

## IPHIGENIA

Ipigenia was the heroine of several Greek legends, and a favorite subject with painters, sculptors, and poets. Her interesting story has been immortalized by two tragedies by Euripides and a play by Schiller; in music, by Gluck; in poetry, by Goethe and Racine. Agamemnon, king of Argos, incurred the wrath of Artemis by killing a deer sacred to her. In revenge she prevented the Greek fleet from sailing to Troy, and would be appeased only upon the condition that Agamemnon sacrifice to her his daughter, Iphigenia. When Iphigenia was brought to the altar she disappeared and a deer lay there in her stead. Artemis carried her off in a cloud to Tauris, where, acting as the priestess of Artemis, Iphigenia sacrificed all strangers in honor of her mistress. In the course of time Orestes, Iphigenia's brother, came there in search of her, but just as she was about to sacrifice him, a happy recognition took place. Orestes then took her, together with the sacred wooden image of Artemis, to Attica.

## IRIS

In Greek mythology Iris was the special golden-winged attendant and messenger of Hera, the queen of heaven, whose commands she executed with tact, intelligence, and swiftness. Iris is usually represented seated behind the chariot of Hera, robed in an airy fabric of variegated hues resembling mother-of-pearl. The rainbow was originally regarded as the path over which she passed to earth, and thus Iris came to be the personification of the rainbow.

## IXION

In Greek mythology Ixion was king of the Lapithae (a mythical race related to the Centaurs). After being admitted to heaven, he attempted to seduce Hera, but Zeus tricked him into embracing a cloud in the shape Hera instead, whereby he became the father of the Centaurs. To punish him for his attempted seduction of Hera, Zeus ordered Hermes to fasten Ixion's hands and feet to an eternally revolving wheel in hell.

## JASON

In Greek legend Jason was king of Iolcus, in Thessaly, who, to regain for his father the throne usurped by his uncle Pelias, organized the Argonautic expedition in quest of the Golden Fleece. Victorious, he returned with his wife, Medea, who helped him to renew the youth of his father and to put to death the wicked Pelias. Jason and Medea then fled to Corinth, where sometime later he deserted her and married Glauce, the daughter of the king of that country. In revenge Medea sent a robe of cloth-of-gold saturated with a deadly poison that penetrated to the flesh of the wearer. The unsuspecting Glauce at once donned the garment, and after horrible sufferings expired. Then Medea slew her three sons. To avenge these deaths Jason started in quest of Medea, who passed over his head, gliding through the air in a golden chariot drawn by dragons. In despair Jason slew himself upon the threshold of his new home.

## LAOCOON

In ancient classic legend, Laocoon was a priest of Poseidon or Apollo who warned his Trojan countrymen
against bringing into the city the wooden horse by
which Troy was captured. The goddess Athena, to
whom the Greeks had consecrated the wooden monster, in revenge for his warning caused two snakes to
come out of the sea. They first twined themselves
around the two sons of Laocoon, and when he vainly
endeavored to save them the serpents attacked him and
crushed him to death.

## LETHE

From the Greek word *lethe,* meaning *forgetfulness,* the
Lethe was, in ancient mythology, one of the five rivers
of Hades. Its waters made those who drank of them
unmindful of the past. Departed spirits before entering
the Elysian Fields drank to forget their earthly cares;
those who were to return to the upper world in new
bodies drank that they might have no recollection of
Elysian joys. The word is used figuratively to denote
oblivion or forgetfulness.

## MEDEA

According to the Greek myths, Medea was a sorceress
who had much to do with the rise to power of Jason.
When he came with his Argonauts to the kingdom of
her father in Colchis, she helped him to obtain the lus-
trous Golden Fleece by putting to sleep the dragon that
guarded it, and then, fearing her father, she fled with the
hero. Her father pursued, and she, to gain time, killed

her young brother Absyrtus and scattered his limbs on the sea. On her arrival in Thessaly she put to death by a stratagem Pelias, Jason's uncle, who had usurped the throne, and she reigned with Jason for many years, foiling his enemies by her arts and advancing his interests in many ways. Jason seems not to have found her a comfortable mate, however, for he deserted her for the young Glauce, and Medea in revenge sent to her rival a poisoned robe, in the folds of which she found an agonizing death. As a climax to her evil life, Medea killed her own children, and then mounting her dragon-car disappeared above the city. The Grecian dramatist Euripides used this story as the plot of one of his greatest tragedies, *Medea,* and it is also the theme of an opera by Cherubini.

### MEDUSA

In Greek legend Medusa was one of three frightful daughters of the sea-god Phorcys. The three sisters were collectively known as the Gorgons, and they lived on the shore of an ocean where the sun never shone. Stheno and Euryale, the two older sisters, were immortal, but Medusa was mortal, and in her youth was very beautiful. She boasted of her beauty to the goddess Athena, who through jealousy changed her into a monster with brazen teeth and claws and with serpents for hair. She became so hideous that all who beheld her were turned into stone. Perseus cut off her head, which Athena placed in the center of her shield.

## MENELAUS

Menelaus, a character in Greek mythology, was a son of Atreus, brother of Agamemnon, and husband of the beautiful Helen of Troy. The happy married life of Menelaus and his wife came to a sudden end when Paris, the son of Priam, king of Troy, visited them, fell in love with Helen, and persuaded her to elope with him to Troy. Menelaus, aided by the Greek chieftains, sought revenge; thus came about the famous Trojan War. After ten years he recovered Helen and started back to Sparta with her, but the two had displeased the gods and were in consequence driven by storms to other shores. At last they reached their native land safely, and there they took up their reign.

## MENTOR

According to ancient legend, when Odysseus went from his home to fight in the Trojan War he left his little son, Telemachus, in the care of Mentor, who was really the goddess Athena in disguise. Mentor proved to be such an excellent guardian that today the word *mentor* denotes a person who gives wise, friendly counsel (to a younger or less experienced person); an experienced, trusted adviser or trainer.

## MIDAS

Midas was a mythical king of Phrygia who had a wondrous garden into which Silenus, an aged woodland deity who educated Dionysus, loved to go. The king, by mixing some poison in a fountain, succeeded in capturing Silenus, whom, after a time, he returned to Dionysus. Pleased at regaining his old tutor, Dionysus conferred upon Midas the power of turning to gold everything he touched. When this power proved a curse, by turning his food to gold, the king sought release from Dionysus and was told that if he bathed in the river Pactolus he would be freed.

Once Midas acted as judge between Apollo and Pan in a musical contest, and decided in favor of the latter. This so enraged Apollo that he caused a pair of ass's ears to grow upon the king's head. Midas tried to conceal the deformity, but a slave discovered it when dressing the ruler's hair. Afraid to tell, yet unable to keep the strange secret, the slave dug a hole in the earth and there whispered his funny tale. Later, reeds grew up over the spot, and whenever the wind blew over them they sang to all passersby, "King Midas has ass's ears."

## MINOS
Minos was a legendary king of Crete, son of Zeus and Europa, who sacrificed Athenian youths and maidens to the Minotaur, a creature half man and half bull, in his labyrinth. For a time he lived in a sacred cave, where he received instruction from Zeus, his father, on how to rule Crete. Celebrated for his administration of justice (despite the above-mentioned sacrifices), after his death he was appointed (along with his brothers, Aeacus and Rhadamanthus) one of the judges of the dead on their descent to the underworld.

## MINOTAUR
The Minotaur was the monster with the head of a bull

and the body of a man that, according to Greek mythology, belonged to King Minos. Once every nine years
seven youths and seven maidens from Athens were sacrificed to it, but on the third occasion the hero Theseus
killed the Minotaur and found his way out of the labyrinth by following a thread that Ariadne, the king's
daughter, had given him.

MUSES

As every river, mountain, and tree had its particular deity, according to the ancient Greeks, so did every art and
science; and the goddesses who presided over these
were called the Muses. They were beautiful maidens,
nine in number, the daughters of Zeus and Memory,
and they were grave or gay according to the special subject over which they presided. Thus Terpsichore and
Thalia, Muses respectively of the dance and of comedy,
were merry of aspect, while Melpomene, the Muse of
tragedy, was of serious mien. At all the feasts of the
gods on Olympus the Muses sang in chorus, often with
Apollo, whose special attendants they were. The Muses
and the departments over which they presided were, in
addition to those mentioned above, Calliope, the de-
partment of epic poetry; Euterpe, lyric poetry; Erato,
love poetry; Polyhymnia, sacred poetry; Clio, history;
and Urania, astronomy.

NAIADS

As the dryads, in classical mythology, presided over
trees and woods, so the naiads were the special divinities
of springs, fountains, brooks, and rivers. They were

greatly venerated, and goats and lambs were sacrificed to them; milk, fruit, and flowers were offered to them, and oil, honey, and wine were poured out as libations.

## NARCISSUS

Narcissus, a character in Greek mythology, was the son of Cephissus, the river god, and Leiriope, a nymph. Narcissus was a handsome lad, very vain of his own beauty, and indifferent to beauty in others. Echo, a nymph, and a favorite of the gods, was so wounded by his rejection of her love that she faded away until only her beautiful voice remained. The gods, angered by Narcissus' coldness and Echo's death, caused him to fall hopelessly in love with his own image, mirrored in a spring. Fascinated by his own face, he bent unceasingly over the spring until he, too, died and was changed by the gods into the flower that bears his name.

## NECTAR

In Greek mythology nectar was the celestial drink of the gods, in which they pledged one another from cups brought by Hebe and Ganymede. It resembled red wine, and with ambrosia, the food of the gods, conferred youth, beauty, and immortality. Mortals were not permitted to drink it.

## NEMESIS

In Greek mythology Nemesis was the goddess of vengeance, who represented the just anger of the gods. She was especially inflexible in her attitude toward those who were proud and insolent and did not pay to the gods proper reverence. Today the word *nemesis* denotes a person or thing that will cause one's downfall or failure; a bitter enemy.

## NEREIDS

According to Greek mythology, the Nereids were the fifty daughters of Nereus and Doris. They were beautiful and friendly sea nymphs, attendants of Poseidon. They were sometimes represented as half human, half fish, but at other times they were pictured as wholly human, riding on seahorses or other monsters of the ocean. Thetis, mother of Achilles, was one of the few well-known Nereids.

## NEREUS

Nereus was a minor deity of the sea. He was famous only as father of the fifty Nereids, and was often called *the old man of the sea.* He alone knew the way to the Garden of the Hesperides, and one of Hercules' twelve labors was to seize the golden apples of the Hesperides. In Hercules' hands, Nereus turned from fire to lion, from lion to water, from water to smoke, until, exhausted, he resumed his own shape and directed the victorious Hercules on his journey.

## ODYSSEUS

In Greek mythology Odysseus (called Ulysses by the Romans) was the king of Ithaca and the most famous of the Greeks in the Trojan War. He was one of the suitors of Helen, and proposed the compact that bound the Greeks to support the husband of Helen, whoever he might be. When he found that he could not be success-ful in his suit for Helen, he married Penelope, the daughter of Icarus, with whom he was very happy. Then he returned to Ithaca, received the crown from his fa-ther, and began to enjoy life in ease and quiet.

When Helen was abducted by Paris, he knew that he would be called upon to fulfill his part of the com-pact, and desiring to remain at home with his wife, he pretended to be insane and spent his time plowing the seashore with a horse and a bull yoked together, and in sowing the shore with salt. But Palamedes suspected the fraud. He put little Telemachus, Odysseus's son, in the furrow, and when Odysseus turned the plow aside to save his child, Palamedes was confirmed in his opinion that the insanity was pretended. He urged upon Odys-seus the binding force of his vow, and Odysseus accord-ingly went to the war.

Throughout the Trojan War he distinguished him-self not only by his great valor but by the wisdom of his counsel and the keenness of his insight into Trojan methods. He fought with Ajax, and won the glorious armor of Achilles. He stole into Troy and assisted Dio-medes in carrying away the Palladium, though in that expedition he did not figure very honorably; and it was he who proposed the building of the Wooden Horse. After the fall of Troy, like most of the Greek chieftains, he suffered many hardships and wandered in many lands, where he had marvelous adventures that formed the subject of Homer's famous *Odyssey*.

On his return, he found his wife faithful to him, though besieged by many suitors. She had persistently put them off by many stratagems, and finally declared that she would accept no one who could not bend the massive bow that her husband had left with her. At this time Odysseus, who had been absent for twenty years, appeared on the scene disguised as a beggar and known only to his son Telemachus and a faithful herdsman. In this guise he entered the room where the suitors were striving to shoot with his own mighty bow. When he asked permission to try his skill, the youths laughed at him, but Telemachus persuaded his mother to let the old man try. To the astonishment of all, Odysseus easily bent the bow and shot the arrow through the twelve rings that she had pointed out. He quickly made himself known, then turning toward the handsomest and most treacherous of the suitors, he shot him through the heart, and by the aid of his son and Athena slew all the other wooers.

ORION

Orion was a hunter who, in Greek mythology, saw and pursued the Pleiades (the seven daughters of Atlas and Pleione), only to lose them. Later he sought to abduct the wife of Oenopion, who detected the scheme, frustrated it, and put out the eyes of Orion. In this pitiful condition, aged and alone, he wandered to the cave of the Cyclopses, who led him to the sun, from whom he borrowed light and youth again. Then Artemis saw him and loved him, and Apollo, angered at what he considered her misplaced affection, challenged his sister to shoot at a black speck far out at sea. She succeeded at the first attempt, and was heartbroken when she learned that the speck was the head of Orion, who had been swimming in the ocean. To assuage her grief, she placed Orion, with his faithful dog Sirius, in the skies as the most beautiful constellation of its part of the heavens.

## PAN

In ancient Greek mythology Pan was the god of pastures, forests, and flocks. He was represented with the head and body of an elderly man, while his lower parts were like the hind quarters of a goat, of which animal he often bore the horns and ears also. He was fond of music and of dancing on his cloven hoofs over glades and mountains, escorted by a bevy of forest nymphs side by side. He was the inventor of the syrinx, or shepherd's flute, hence called *Pans's pipes*. Sudden terror without visible or reasonable cause was attributed to his influence. The modern devil is invested with some of his attributes, such as cloven hoofs.

## PANDORA

Pandora, in Greek mythology, was the first woman created. Zeus was so angered at Prometheus because the latter had stolen fire from heaven that he resolved to avenge himself upon man. So he called upon Hephaestus to fashion a being in godlike form from earth and water. All the gods joined in endowing the new bring with attractive qualities or those qualified to make mischief. Athena gave her artist-knowledge, Aphrodite contributed beauty, and Hermes made her artful and designing. The Graces and the Seasons clothed her, and Zeus christened her Pandora, or *all-gifts*. Thus crowned, the new creation was sent to Prometheus. who received her coldly, for he was suspicious of gifts from the gods. Then Hermes took her to Epimetheus, who was much more trustful than his brother. He married her and was happy until Hermes brought a box that he confided to the care of Pandora, with strict injunctions that she should not open it. Her curiosity, however, was too strong, and she undid the fastenings. Then at once there burst out all the vices, sins, crimes, and sufferings that can afflict man, for Zeus had seen that the box was well filled. Frightened at what she had done, Pandora hastily shut down the lid in time to retain and preserve for man Hope, which always follows suffering and is the chief consoler of the race. (The tale is told in Part IV: Five Selected Myths.)

## PEGASUS

Pegasus was the mythical winged steed that was fashioned by Poseidon from the blood that trickled into the sea from the head of Medusa, as Perseus flew across bearing his hideous burden. At his birth, the horse flew to Mount Helicon, where he created the fountain Hippocrene with a blow of his hoof. Often he came to drink at the fountain of Pirene, and here Bellerophon, bearing the golden bridle given him by Athena, found the animal grazing. At the sight of the bridle, Pegasus yielded himself captive and bore his master away to his successful battle with the Chimaera. After throwing the aged and conceited Bellerophon, Pegasus flew away to the skies and was made the constellation that bears his name.

## PERSEPHONE

Persephone (called Proserpina by the Romans) was the daughter of Demeter, goddess of agriculture. Herself the special protector of flowers, Persephone spent much time in the meadows attending to her favorites. One day while she was engaged in this pleasant task, the god Hades came by in his chariot, drawn by his coal-black horses. Seeing Persephone, with whom he had long been in love, thus unprotected, Hades soiled her and bore her off in his chariot down to his underground home. In vain the girl begged for release, and at length gave up hope of returning to the upper world and the light of the sun.

Meanwhile, Demeter had sought everywhere for her beloved daughter, and when she at last discovered her whereabouts she obtained from Zeus and the Fates a promise that Persephone might return if no food had passed her lips while she was in Hades' realm. When Hermes went to bring her back to earth, however, he found that she had eaten six pomegranate seeds, and in consequence of this she was obliged to spend half of her time each year with her gloomy husband underground. During each six months that she was permitted to be above ground, vegetation flourished; but during the rest of the year winter reigned. This is one of the old myths that accounts for the change in seasons. (The tale is told in Part IV: Five Selected Myths.)


## PHAEDRA

Phaedra, in Grecian myth, was a daughter of Minos and sister of Ariadne. Though he had abandoned Ariadne,

Theseus, in his old age, proposed for the hand of Phaedra and was accepted; but when the young bride came to Athens, she fell in love, not with Theseus, but with his young son, Hippolytus. When he spurned her advances, she accused him to his father of insulting her. The old king prayed to Poseidon to punish his ungrateful son, and Poseidon answered his prayer very promptly, drowning, with his waves, the young prince, who was at that time driving his chariot by the seashore. Phaedra, in a fit of remorse, hanged herself.

PHAETHON

Phaethon, in Greek mythology, was the son of Apollo and Clymene. Clymene had refused to tell her son who his father was until the boy, shamed by his companions, made an imperious demand. When he learned that he was actually the child of the sun god, he boasted of it proudly, and was laughed at by his playmates. To prove his claim, he journeyed to the palace of the sun and asked of his father a sign of his sonship. Apollo promised to grant any request he might make, but when Phaethon demanded that he be allowed to drive the chariot of the sun for one day, the father tried to retract his promise. Phaethon persisted, however, and after cautioning him to drive slowly and to take care to go neither too high nor too low, Apollo reluctantly watched him depart. The rash boy used the whip on his fiery steeds, which tore up the heavens, dragging the chariot after them. They went so high that the earth beneath them almost perished with cold; then they rushed down so close to the earth that vegetation was scorched, rivers were dried up, and rocks were split. The poor Earth called on Zeus for help, and he hurled his thunderbolts at the boy, who fell from the chariot and was killed. (The tale is told in Part IV: Five Selected Myths.)

## POSEIDON

The god Poseidon (called Neptune by the Roman) was the brother of Zeus and second only to him in authority. When the universe was divided, Poseidon received the seas, the rivers and the fountains—in fact the waters everywhere. Two stories of Poseidon were great favorites with the Greeks. The first describes the contest between him and Athena, in which the one who created the more useful object would be privileged to name the new and growing city of Athens. Poseidon created the horse, and pointed out proudly the many ways in which it would be useful to man; but Athena made the olive tree and convinced the judges that it was the more valuable of the two. From her name, the city was called Athens.

At another time, Poseidon, dissatisfied with his kingdom, attempted to gain control of Zeus's, and as punishment was condemned to build for Laomedon, king of Troy, the walls of his city. Apollo aided Poseidon by playing on his lyre, so that the stones sprang into place, and the task was quickly completed. The treacherous king, however, refused to give to the two gods the promised payment, and in consequence both Poseidon and Apollo fought against the city in the Trojan War. Poseidon was especially worshiped by sailors and those who had to do with horses, and games were celebrated in his honor, the most important being the Isthmian Games, which were held every four years at Corinth. In art Poseidon is shown as a majestic man with broad chest and well-developed muscles; in his hand he carries a three-pronged spear, or trident, his special symbol. He is usually drawn through the water by dolphins, and Triton, his son by Amphitrite, accompanies him.

## PROTESILAUS
In Greek mythology Protesilaus was one of the chiefs who joined in the expedition against Troy. An oracle had foretold that the first Greek who attempted to land would meet death immediately; and Protesilaus, seeing that the other chiefs hesitated, leaped ashore and was instantly slain.

## PROTEUS
Proteus, in Greek mythology, was one of the lesser gods of the sea, who possessed the gift of prophecy and had in common with all the gods the power of changing to any shape in which he wished to appear. When asked to prophesy, he invariably refused, and to startle the questioner changed rapidly through a bewildering variety of forms. To those who persisted in their questioning, however, he always in the end gave an answer.

## PSYCHE
Psyche, in Greek mythology, was a princess whose beauty was so great that it aroused the jealousy of the goddess Aphrodite, who called her son Eros and ordered him either to kill Psyche or to make her fall in

love with some hideous wretch. When the youthful god saw the beautiful maiden, he fell in love with her himself and made her his wife. He kept her in a beautiful palace and visited her every night, but she never saw him, for he had told her that if she once looked upon him he should be obliged to leave her forever. For a long time they were very happy, but at last Psyche's jealous sisters convinced her that her invisible husband was a frightful monster and persuaded her to kill him in his sleep. That night Psyche crept up to him with a lighted lamp in one hand and a dagger in the other; and when, by the light of the lamp, she saw the beautiful god, she was so startled that a drop of the burning oil fell upon his shoulder and awakened him. Seeing her standing over him with her dagger, he guessed her intentions and with a reproachful word vanished out of sight, leaving her distracted with grief.

Far and wide she sought him without avail, and many were the difficult tasks that were laid on her by Aphrodite. At last she was sent by this hard-hearted deity to the underground realm to obtain from Persephone some of the latter's fabled beauty. On her return journey curiosity overcame her and she opened the box, only to be overcome by poisonous fumes. Eros came upon her as she lay asleep by the roadside, forgave her, and after much pleading reconciled his mother to the reunion and took her up to Olympus, where she was made immortal. As Eros represents the heart, Psyche was thought to typify the human soul, and the trials through which she went were symbolic of the struggles through which the soul must go before it is made pure.

## PYGMALION

Pygmalion was a mythical Grecian sculptor who became so disgusted with the wickedness of the women of his native town that he scorned them all and refused to marry. All the love that he should have given to a woman went to his art, and as a punishment Aphrodite decreed that he should fall in love with a statue of Galatea that he had carved. So great did this love become that Aphrodite in response to his prayers endowed the statue with life, and the nymph then became Pygmalion's wife.

## PYTHON

Python was a famous serpent that, in a Greek myth, was said to have been born from the mud and foul waters that remained on the earth after Deucalion's flood. This hideous monster lived near Delphi, and preyed upon the cattle and even the people of the surrounding country. Apollo, when he came to Delphi, killed the animal with his arrows, and thereafter the place and the oracle of Apollo were given the name of Pytho. Originally this was a nature myth; the poisonous serpent was the miasmatic fog from the winding swamp, which was dispersed by the sun's rays. The sun was represented by Apollo.

## RHADAMANTHUS

Rhadamanthus was a son of Zeus and Europa. By his inflexible integrity he aroused the jealousy of his brother Minos, while the latter was king of Crete, and was forced to flee from the country. After his death Rhadamanthus and his brothers, Minos and Aeacus, ruled as judges of the lower world. It was their duty to question all newly arrived souls, to sort out the good thoughts and actions from the bad, and to place them in the scales of Themis, the goddess of justice. If the good outweighed the evil the spirit went to the Elysian Fields; if evil prevailed, the spirit suffered in the fires of Tartarus.

## RHEA

In classic mythology Rhea was a goddess who was the symbol of the productiveness of nature. She was often given the name of "Mother of the Gods." Rhea was the daughter of Uranus and Gaea, or Heaven and Earth, the sister and wife of Cronus, the mother of Hades, Zeus, Poseidon, Hera, Hestea, and Demeter. In Phrygia, a division of Asia Minor, Rhea was identified with Cybele, who presided over mountain refuges and fortified places. She was attended by priests called Curetes, and her chariot was driven by lions. Rhea cured Dionysus of madness, taught him her religious rites, then sent him forth to teach the cultivation of the vine.

## SATYR

In Greek mythology a satyr was a god of the woods, who had a man's head and hairy body, but the ears, legs, and feet of a goat. Satyrs are associated with the worship of Bacchus (Dionysus), and appear in the chorus of the dramas acted at the Bacchic festivals. Pan was the chief of the satyrs.

## SCYLLA AND CHARYBDIS

Scylla, in Greek mythology, was a famous, six-headed sea monster who was once a beautiful maiden but was changed by Circe because of the latter's jealousy. She lived in a cave in a great cliff, so high that the top could never be seen. It was her custom to thrust her heads out of the cave and seize the animals and men that passed. From every ship each head took toll. Opposite the cliff of Scylla was Charybdis, another monster who continually drew in the water and threw it out again. The ancients located the rock Scylla and the whirlpool Charybdis in the strait of Messina. The difficulty of steering between the rock and the whirlpool gave rise to a popular expression "between Scylla and Charybdis," as indicating two dangers, or evils, one of which must be chosen.

## SEMELE

In Greek mythology, Semele was a beautiful daughter of Cadmus. She was wooed and won by Zeus in the guise of a mortal, but the jealous Hera, taking the form of Semele's nurse, induced her to ask of Zeus that he appear before her in his divine glory. First she extracted from Zeus a promise to grant any favor to her she might ask, and then she made her request. In vain the king of the gods protested; Semele was firm, and Zeus at last was obliged to yield to her entreaties. He donned only his mildest glory, but even this was too much for the mortal eyes of Semele, who was burned to death in the blaze of light that surrounded him. Dionysus, her son, was caught up by his father and saved from destruction.

## SIBYL
In Greek mythology, a sibyl was a prophetess who owed her divine gift to Apollo. The most famous was the *Cumaean sibyl,* who, so the story goes, appeared before King Tarquin the Proud and offered him nine books for sale. This offer he refused, and a second offer, after she had destroyed three books, was also declined. When she appeared before him the third time, with but three books left, he bought them, paying the price she had asked for the nine. These three books were kept in the temple of Zeus, and when it was burned in 83 B.C. they were likewise destroyed.

## SILENUS
Silenus, in Greek mythology, was a demigod, the most distinguished of the satyrs. He was the nurse, teacher and follower of Dionysus. He is represented as very fat, bald, and pug-nosed, riding on a broad-backed ass. He is usually pictured as intoxicated, swaying about, and brandishing his drinking cup.

## SIRENS
In Greek mythology, the Sirens were two maidens who lived on an island and by their exquisite singing enticed mariners to their shore, where they remained, forgetful of home, of friends, and of duty until they died of starvation. Odysseus was warned by Circe of the danger from the Sirens, and he stopped the ears of his companions with wax. He himself wished to hear the music, but

81

he had himself strapped to the mast of his vessel so that he could not yield to the charm if he wished to.

## SISYPHUS
Sisyphus was a mythical king of Corinth, in ancient Greece. He was one of the most crafty of men, and his schemes puzzled even the gods. When Zeus carried off Aegina, Sisyphus told her father who had done the deed, and in consequence Zeus sent Death to punish the informer. But Sisyphus outwitted Death and bound him in fetters, so that there was great rejoicing all over the earth, for no man died. Hades set Death at liberty, and Sisyphus was given into the hands of Death. With his dying breath Sisyphus begged his wife not to bury his body, and when he had gone to the underworld he complained to Hades of the mistreatment, and begged permission to go back to earth and punish his wife for her neglect. Hades consented, and as soon as Sisyphus was again in his own house, he refused to return. Hermes, however, led him back, and when Hades had him once more in the underworld, he condemned him thereafter to the task of rolling up a high hill a large stone that ever rolled down again.

## HYPNOS
Hypnos (called Somnus by the Romans) was the god of sleep, and the son of Erebus and Nyx. He dwelt in a great cave in a remote and quiet valley with his brother Thanatos, the god of death. Shadowy forms kept watch about the mouth of the cave, and shook great bunches of poppies, while they enjoined silence upon all who

came near. In one of the darkened inner rooms of the cave drowsy Hypnos lay upon his couch, clothed in black garments studded with stars. On his head was a crown of poppies, and in his hand a goblet of poppy juice. Morpheus, his son, supported his head and protected him during his slumbers. Pleasant Dreams hovered about his couch, and hideous Nightmares lurked in the darkened corners. Sometimes the Dreams were sent out of this valley by way of glittering ivory gates to the earth, where they warned mortals of coming misfortunes.

SPHINX

In Grecian mythology the sphinx was a wicked being usually represented as a lion, having the head of a woman, the tail of a serpent, and the wings of a bird. This creature lived in a cliff just outside the city of Thebes, and kept guard over the road to the city. To every passerby she put this riddle: What animal is it that walks on four legs in the morning, two at noon, and three in the evening? And anyone who failed to answer correctly was immediately devoured. When Oedipus passed on the way to Thebes, the riddle was put to him, and without much hesitation he declared the animal to be man, who walked on his hands and feet when young, erect on his two feet in middle life, and with the aid of a staff in old age. With a howl of rage because her riddle had been answered correctly, the sphinx hurled herself from the rocks and was killed.

## STYX

The Styx, in Greek mythology, was the dark, dreary river that flowed seven times around Hades, the abode of the dead. Across it the departed spirits were rowed by the ferryman Charon, to the realms of Hades, who assigned them either to the Elysian Fields or to the grim regions of Tartarus. A lofty waterfall in Arcadia was also known as the Styx. Its waters were supposed to be poisonous and its barren surroundings suggested the entrance to the lower world.

## TANTALUS

Tantalus, in mythology, was a Grecian king who was said to be the son of Zeus and the father of Pelops and Niobe. According to legend he killed his son Pelops and served him as a dish to the gods, who in punishment condemned Tantalus to terrible sufferings in Hades. Plagued by an unquenchable thirst, he was made to stand immersed to the chin in water, which always receded when he tried to drink; and gnawed by never-ceasing hunger, he saw hanging above him fruit-laden branches, which always swung away when he tried to reach them. From this legend the word *tantalize* is derived.

## TARTARUS

In early Greek mythology, Tartarus was a dark abyss surrounded by the fiery river Phlegethon, where Zeus imprisoned the rebelling Titans. Tartarus was later considered the place of punishment for all spirits of the wicked, and the name was used interchangeably with

Hades. Aeneas, in his adventures in the abode of dead souls, comes to a point where the road divides, the right branch leading to Elysium and the left to Tartarus.

## TELEMACHUS
In Greek legend Telemachus was the son of Odysseus and Penelope. When he reached manhood, he visited Pylos and Sparta to make inquiries about his father, who had been absent for nearly twenty years. On his return, he found that Odysseus had reached home before him. Then father and son, aided by Eumaeus and Philoetius, slew or drove out the suitors of Penelope. According to later tradition, Telemachus became the husband of Circe and by her the father of Latinus and of a daughter Roma, afterwards the wife of Aeneas. In another story, he married a daughter of Circe, named Cassiphone; having slain his mother-in-law in a quarrel, he was himself killed by his wife.

## TERPSICHORE
Terpsichore (pronounced terp-SIK-oh-ree) was one of the nine Muses, the patron of dancing, which she is said to have originated. In the last days of the Greek religion her attributions became restricted chiefly to the province of lyric poetry. In art she is represented as a laurel-crowned virgin of graceful figure, clad in flowing draperies, often seated, and usually holding a lyre.

## THESEUS
Theseus was a famous legendary king of Athens, whose marvelous exploits formed themes for Grecian poets,

and whose wise and benevolent rule established the original power of Athens. He was the son of Aegeus and Aethra, and was brought up in seclusion by his mother until he became a man. Then he removed the heavy stone that his father had placed over the sword and sandals by which he was to recognize his son, took his legacy and proceeded to Athens. Arrived there, he found his father much under the influence of his wife Medea, who when she saw Theseus recognized as heir to the king, tried to poison him. Upon the failure of her attempt she fled in her dragon-car to Media, never to return.

When Theseus learned of the terrible *tribute* (payment made from one state or ruler to another) Athens was compelled to pay to King Minos of Crete (in the form of seven youths and seven maidens, to be sacrificed), he volunteered to go as part of the sacrifice for that year and, if possible, to kill the Minotaur, whose savage lust for human flesh had to be gratified. Aegeus pleaded in vain, and Theseus set sail in the black-sailed vessel for Crete. He killed the Minotaur, with the aid of Ariadne, the king's daughter, and with her and his joyous companions set sail for Greece. As a punishment for his crime in deserting Ariadne on the return home, Theseus was made to forget to change his vessel's sails from black to white, the agreed sign of the success of his expedition, and in consequence suffered the loss of his father, who killed himself.

On his arrival at Athens he was proclaimed king and entered at once on the beneficent policy that made the city great. After years of prosperous rule, however, he became cruel and overbearing, and was driven by his people into exile. Too late they realized how great a man he had been; and they brought back his remains to the city and buried them in a beautiful temple where the hero was worshiped as a god.

## TITANS

In Greek mythology, the Titans were the giant sons and daughters of Uranus (Heaven) and Gaea (Earth). Six of them were men, and six were women. The latter were called the Titanides. So strong were the Titans that Uranus greatly feared them and threw them from Olympus down into a dark cavern in the earth called Tartarus, where he chained them fast. Gaea grieved over the loss of her children, and urged her husband to set them free; but whenever he heard their angry roars he renewed his determination to keep them where they were.

Finally Gaea grew very angry, and herself descended into Tartarus, where she urged the Titans to revenge themselves upon their father, but all refused to undertake the heavy task excepting Cronus, the youngest. Gaea gave him a scythe, released him from his chains, and ordered him set forth against his father. Meeting the latter unawares, Cronus defeated him by means of the wonderful scythe, and wounded him severely. So angry was Uranus that he cursed his son and prophesied that some day he, too, would be overthrown by his own child. Cronus released his brothers and sisters, all of whom consented to his ruling. He selected Rhea for his wife, and assigned to each of the others some portion of the earth. Later Zeus overthrew Cronus, and those Titans who did not submit willingly to his rule were again confined in Tartarus.

## TYCHE

Tyche (called Fortuna by the Romans) was the goddess of chance, correspond. She differed from Destiny, or Fate, in that she dispensed joy or sorrow at her own pleasure, and without regard to law. In Greek art she is usually represented with a rudder, indicating her guiding power; with a cornucopia, as a symbol of prosperity; or with a ball, wheel, or wings, typifying her fickle character.

## URANIA

Urania was the one of the nine Muses who was known as the patron of astronomy and celestial forces. She is generally represented with a crown of stars, in a garment spotted with stars. In one hand she holds a celestial globe and in the other a little staff or compass for indicating the course of the stars.

## URANUS

In Greek mythology Uranus, meaning Heaven, was the most ancient of the gods, the personification of the sky. He was the husband of Gaea (Earth) and by her the father of the Cyclopses, the Titans, and the terrible hundred-handed giants. Uranus was deposed from his throne by Cronus, the youngest of the Titans, and killed; from his blood sprang the Furies.

## WOODEN HORSE

After the Trojan War had gone on for ten years, it became clear to the Greeks that if they were to take Troy,
it must be through stratagem and not through force, and
the wily Odysseus was called upon to furnish a plan. On
his advice the Greeks built a huge wooden horse, which
they filled with Greek warriors and left upon the plains
before Troy. Then the army took to their ships and hid
themselves behind an island, out of sight of the city.
The Trojans, finding the large and curious object, fell
into a violent discussion as to whether or not it should
be taken into the city, and were induced by the disaster
that befell Laocoon to receive it within their walls. They
also took into the city Sinon, a Greek slave, who had
been left behind for that very purpose. After nightfall
Sinon released the imprisoned Greeks from the horse,
and these in turn opened the gates of the city to the
Greek soldiers, who had quietly returned. The city was
then easily captured and destroyed

## ZEUS

Zeus (called Jupiter by the Romans) was the mythological king of heaven. Having by strength and cleverness
brought about the overthrow of his father, Cronus, he
divided the world with his two brothers, giving to Hades
the underworld, to Poseidon the sea, and reserving for
himself the sky, with supreme sovereignty over gods and
men. He married first the goddess of wisdom, Metis,
but becoming alarmed by a prophecy that his first child
should be wiser than its father, he swallowed his wife.
This precaution proved vain, however, for shortly af-

terward there sprang from his head, full grown, the goddess Athena, whose name became a synonym for wisdom of the highest kind.

As his wife, and the queen of heaven, Zeus selected Hera, but her jealousy and dignity irked him at times, and he solaced himself with many other wives, both among the goddesses and among mortals. To him were born many children, of whom the most famous were Apollo and his twin sister Artemis, Ares, Hebe, the Fates, and the Muses.

Greek artists represented this greatest of their gods as a bearded man of middle age, handsome and majestic and generally benignant. Beside him perched the eagle, his strong-winged messenger, and in his hands were grasped the thunderbolts with which he punished gods and men.

# 3 ABOUT THE TROJAN WAR, THE *ILIAD,* AND THE *ODYSSEY*

## *ABOUT THE TROJAN WAR*

In the days of Priam, the king, Troy became a great city, but there were signs of approaching disaster. When Prince Paris was born it was foretold that he should bring trouble to his country, and to avoid this the royal father ordered the boy to be exposed on the hillside to die. The servants did his bidding, but scarcely had they gone when an old shepherd found the beautiful boy and carried him to his home. There Paris grew up as the shepherd's son, tending the flocks of his foster-father on Mount Ida.

When Paris had become a young man, handsome as a god, there occurred a wonderful wedding, to which no one thought of inviting him. It was the wedding of the sea nymph Thetis with Peleus, and to it came all the immortals except Eris, goddess of discord. To avenge the slight shown her, Eris threw among the guests a golden apple bearing the inscription, "For the fairest of the fair," and she accomplished her purpose, for out of it arose a wrangle that resulted in the disastrous siege of Troy. Aphrodite, Hera, and Athena all jealously claimed the apple, and a most unseemly quarrel ensued, of which Paris was finally chosen as judge.

All three goddesses appeared before him on Mount Ida, each offering him a bribe if he would decide for her: "I will give you power and riches," declared Hera. "I will make you a famous warrior," said the martial Athena. "I shall give you the most beautiful woman on earth for your wife," smiled Aphrodite.

Not because of her promise, but because she was really the most beautiful, Paris gave the apple to Aphrodite. He needed no beautiful wife, for he had already wedded the nymph Oenone, whom he loved; but by his decision he won not only the hatred of Hera and Athena, but the still more disastrous favor of Aphrodite.

Very shortly Paris was recalled to his father's palace, and soon afterward set out on a journey to Sparta, in Greece, urged on by Aphrodite, though this he did not know. There he met Helen, wife of the Spartan king Menelaus, and the most beautiful woman on earth, and with her he fell in love. Through the influence of Aphrodite, Helen returned his love. Whether she consented to flee with him to Troy or he abducted her, there is doubt; but she went, forgetting apparently that all the heroes of Greece had promised to aid her husband if any disaster ever overtook him. The heroes were true to their oath, and preparations for the expedition began immediately after the flight.

They were not made in a moment, these extensive preparations, and many difficulties stood in the way of the Greeks. First Odysseus, wisest of the Greeks, had to be induced to join the expedition; then Agamemnon, the Greek commander-in-chief, had to placate Artemis by the sacrifice of his daughter Iphigenia, but finally the fleet set sail for Troy, where preparations had also been in progress.

For nine years the struggle went on with varying fortunes. The Trojans were compelled to shut themselves up within their city, but beyond that the invaders were able to accomplish nothing. Then came the "ruinous wrath" of Achilles, greatest of Greek heroes, which was almost fatal to the Grecian cause and which he was induced only by the death of his friend Patroclus to lay aside. With Achilles once more fighting for them, the Greeks felt a return of confidence; and when Hector, the noble hero of Troy, was killed, it seemed as if their victory was won. But Achilles himself was put to death soon afterward by the treacherous Paris, and matters were again at a standstill.

But the crafty Odysseus devised a plan. He induced the Greeks to build a gigantic wooden horse and to conceal in it a body of armed men, while all the rest of the Greeks took to their ships, apparently with the intention of sailing for home. The stratagem was successful. The curious Trojans, despite the warnings of Laocoon, priest of Poseidon, dragged the wonderful horse within the city walls, and in the night the armed men crept out and let into the city the Greek forces, which had stolen back under cover of the darkness. The terrified Trojans rushed from their houses only to fall by the swords of the Greeks, and in a brief time the whole city was in flames.

So fell Troy. The Greeks could claim for themselves no proud victory, since it was by craft and not by valor that the long siege was ended.

## ABOUT THE ILIAD

The *Iliad*, regarded by many as the greatest epic in the world, is ascribed to the ancient Greek poet, Homer. Whether Homer wrote it, or whether it is actually a folk-epic built up through generation after generation and given its final form by Homer; whether, indeed, there ever lived such a person as Homer—these questions have been studied by some of the world's greatest scholars, and are still unanswered. The quantity of literature that has grown up about this one poem is enormous, and still men's interest in it continues.

The *Iliad* describes an episode covering about 40 days in the 10 years' siege of Troy by the Greeks. In order to understand the *Iliad*, the facts leading up to it, some of which are mentioned in the poem, must be known. The Trojan Paris had carried off the fairest woman in Greece—Helen, wife of Menelaus, king of Sparta. She had been given to Paris by the goddess Aphrodite as a reward for his having decided in her favor the triangular contest of beauty between herself, Athena, and Hera.

To recover Helen and avenge the wrong, the

Greeks, under command of Agamemnon, king of Mycenae, and brother of Menelaus, had set sail in 1,100 ships to besiege Troy. Ten years they besieged the city without result, for the Trojans would not venture forth to combat on account of their dread of the famous hero, Achilles. Finally, Achilles suffered insult from Agamemnon, who took from him the captive maiden Briseis, who had been assigned to him after the sack of a small outlying town. Achilles left the conflict and withdrew to his tent by the seashore. This is the point at which the *Iliad* begins, and much of the poem is devoted to the "Wrath of Achilles," its causes, effects, and how it was appeased.

The Trojans now come forth to meet the Greeks, and fifteen of the twenty-four books of the *Iliad* tell the varying fortunes of the conflict. (The *Iliad* is divided into twenty-four sections called "books," with each book usually representing a distinct episode in the plot.) Finally in Book XVI, Patroclus begs Achilles to lend him his armor, and with it goes into battle. The Trojans believe they see Achilles, and flee in terror, but at length Patroclus is afflicted with a stupor by Apollo, and is slain by Hector.

To avenge his friend, Achilles returns to the combat, with a new suit of armor given him from Hephaestus. Achilles slays Hector and drags his body to the ships. In the last book King Priam begs of Achilles his son's body, and during a truce Hector is buried with fitting rites. The struggle is watched by the gods throughout the poem. Ares and Apollo aid the Trojans; Hera, Athena, and the other deities, the Greeks. Several famous single combats occur, as between Paris and Menelaus in Book III, Hector and Ajax in Book VII, Aeneas and Achilles in Book XX.

The value of the *Iliad* is not simply that it tells a fascinating story in a straightforward, simple way, nor that its thought is consistently lofty and its lines swinging and majestic; it is, in addition to all this, a record of antiquity, and very much that is known about the modes of life and of thought in those faraway times has been learned from its pages.

## ABOUT THE ODYSSEY

The *Odyssey,* usually considered the work of the Greek poet Homer, describes the wanderings and sufferings of Odysseus, one of the Greek heroes, on his return from the Trojan War. At the beginning of his voyage he is wrecked on the coast of Thrace, and in plundering the town of Ismarus, he loses many of his followers.

Next he was driven to the coast of Libya, and from there northward to the goat island. With one ship he sailed to the island of the Cyclopses, on the west coast of Sicily. Odysseus and twelve companions entered the cave of the one-eyed monster, Polyphemus, who devoured six of the intruders. Odysseus makes Polyphemus drunk with wine, blinds him with a burning pole and escapes with his comrades.

Henceforth Odysseus was pursued by the wrath of Poseidon, whose son, the Cyclops, he had blinded. After losing all his ships but one, he reaches an island where dwells the sorceress Circe, who counsels him to make a journey to Hades.

After that, he sailed by the island of the enticing, beautiful-voiced Sirens, and after successfully passing between the monster Scylla and the whirlpool Charybdis, reaches Thrinacia, the island of Helios. Here his companions killed some sacred oxen and consequently on their next voyage were all shipwrecked and drowned. Odysseus escaped to the island where lived the nymph Calypso, and remained there eight years.

Leaving there on a raft he was again wrecked, but reached Scheria, the island of the Phaeacians. The princess Nausicaa and her maidens discover him, and he is kindly received and cared for by King Alcinous. After a happy sojourn he is sent to Ithaca, and after slaying the suitors of his wife Penelope, is gladly welcomed by her and all his subjects.

The *Odyssey,* like the *Iliad,* is in twenty-four books. Though, like the other great epic, it is attributed to Homer, the same question as to its real authorship exists. By many scholars it is believed that the *Odyssey* is an outgrowth of the tales of early navigators who dared the dangers of the Mediterranean, though it is by no means certain that it has even that basis in history. However that may be, it remains one of the world's great classics, and a tale of absorbing interest to those who love to read of adventure.

# 4 FIVE SELECTED GREEK MYTHS

## *I. THE STORY OF PERSEPHONE*

Demeter, the goddess of agriculture, was one of the busiest of the deities. In the springtime, she had to go about from field to field all over the earth, attending to the sowing of the seeds; in the summer, she watched the growth of the grains and fruits; and in the autumn, she went about from place to place blessing the harvests. Her car bore her swiftly, and she so loved the helpful work she did that she never grew tired. Still, she was always glad to come back to her home and to her beautiful daughter, Persephone, whom she loved very dearly.

Like her mother, Persephone had her duties to perform, though they were not as difficult as those of her mother. She had charge of all the flowers, and in the springtime, when she walked across the meadows, violets and daisies and buttercups sprang up in her footsteps. Naturally, she loved the flowers, and spent much of her time in the fields with her companions tending them and gathering them for wreaths.

One day, as Persephone and her friends played in the meadows, they heard a strange, rumbling sound and looked up hastily. A huge, dark chariot with dark horses and a handsome, but gloomy-looking driver was coming toward them. The girls screamed in terror and started to scatter. But the driver stopped his chariot, leaped to the ground, and seizing Persephone, bore her away with him in his chariot. The frightened girl called to her companions and to her mother, but the black horses carried them on too swiftly for any help to follow her. Meanwhile the stern-looking man explained to Persephone that he was Hades, king of all the regions below the earth; that he loved her and wanted her for his wife.

Persephone answered, "I must tell my mother; she will be wild with grief when she finds that I am gone and knows not where to look for me."

But Hades shook his head. "She would never let you go with me," he declared.

While they were talking thus, they had come to the margin of the River Cyane, which opposed their passage. Angrily, Hades struck the ground with the great trident that he carried, and the earth opened and made him a passage back to his underground kingdom.

The darkness in which they found themselves after the earth had closed behind them was delightful to Hades, whose eyes were tired with the glare of the sun; but to Persephone it was nothing less than horrible. All her life she had been used to living out-of-doors from daylight to dark; and now this was far, far worse than the blackest night she had ever seen.

"You will like it when you become accustomed to it." said Hades, noticing that the girl trembled as she sat beside him.

Gradually the way grew lighter, though the light was white and ghostly—not like the beautiful golden sunlight of the upper world.

When they came at length to the huge palace of Hades, he expected Persephone to exclaim with delight over its gorgeousness; for Hades owned all the gold and silver and gems that lay hidden in the earth and had made good use of them in decking his palace. But Persephone was not used to gorgeousness. She and her mother had lived simply always, and the rich gems that she saw about her were less to her than a handful of fragrant flowers would have been. And all the jewel-studded lights, which to her seemed to serve only to make the gloom more noticeable, she would have exchanged for one look at the stars.

It was the same way with the food. All her life she had eaten but the plainest dishes — simple grains, fruits, bread, and milk. And the rich food that Hades ordered to be placed before her seemed so strange to her that she would not even taste It. This went on for several days. Hades, in great distress, urging her to eat, and she as steadily refusing.

Meanwhile her mother had been almost distracted with fear and grief. The girls with whom Persephone had been playing could tell her nothing except that a man in a black chariot had carried off her daughter. Who the man was, she could have no idea. She sought day and night through one country after another for her daughter. The sun, when he came through the doors of the East in the morning, saw her wandering on, stopping everyone to inquire for her lost girl, and the evening star found her still at her task. One day, as she sat for a few minutes resting on a stone, an old man with a little girl passed her. The goddess bore about her no signs of her divinity; she looked like a poor, worn-out, old woman, and they took pity on her and begged her to go home with them. At last she consented to do so, and as they walked the old man told her that his little son was very sick of a fever and that he feared to find him dead.

When they reached the house they found that the child had grown rapidly worse, that he was, in fact, almost dead. You may imagine the delight it caused when Demeter, taking the child in her arms, kissed him and thus restored him instantly to health. Then she asked that she might be allowed to take charge of the boy. Of course, the family was only too glad to have so excellent a nurse; but the mother, overanxious for the son in whose sudden recovery she could scarcely yet believe, determined to hide and watch what happened; and it was, indeed, a startling sight that she saw.

Demeter bathed the boy, murmured some magic-sounding words over him, and then, stepping to the hearth, raked a hollow in the glowing coals and laid the boy within it. The watching mother sprang forward with a cry and snatched her child from what she believed would have been its death. But what was her amazement, when she turned around, to see before her

101

not the feeble old woman whom her husband had brought home, but the radiant goddess Demeter, with her hair of gold and of wheat and scarlet poppies.

Demeter spoke sadly, but not angrily. "I would have given to your son," she said, "immortality. Now you, by your failure to trust me, have taken from him that gift." And with these words,, the goddess vanished.

Her search still continued, and finally, when it seemed that everything was in vain, Demeter became angry with the earth that had failed to aid her in her search and laid her curse upon it. Drought and famine, she declared, should extend over the whole earth; nothing green should grow; there should be no seedtime, no harvest, until her daughter should come back to her. In vain the people implored her, in vain tales of their suffering came to her ears; she, usually so gracious and kindly, was cruel enough now.

At length she found a clew. The river Arethusa, which comes up from the underworld, had in the kingdom of the underworld a queen who looked, she said, most like Persephone. She was pale and sad, and the white poppies that she wore in her hair were very different from the bright flowers she had been so fond of wearing. But still, beyond a doubt, thought the river Arethusa, it was Persephone. Demeter knew not whether to be glad or sorry. Her daughter was found, but found where? She went to the meeting place of the gods on Olympus, which she had not visited since the loss of her daughter, and implored Zeus to use some means to have her daughter brought to her. All the gods felt sorry for Demeter, and they felt sorry, moreover, for the people on the earth, whom Demeter's grief was causing to suffer. At length Zeus summoned Hermes, the messenger of the gods, and sent him to the regions of the underworld.

"I will do my best," said the king of gods and men, "but the Fates are even stronger than I, and they have declared that if your daughter has eaten anything while she has been in Hades's realm, she may not again come back to the light of day."

When Hermes reached the kingdom of Hades and stood before the king and the sad-eyed queen, he himself felt sorry for her and hoped that he should be able to take her back with him. When it became known, however, that Persephone had eaten a few of the seeds of a pomegranate, Hermes shook his head in despair. "It cannot be," he said, and he went sadly back to the assembly of the gods, leaving Persephone more hopeless than before.

At length, however, the Fates agreed to make a decree less severe, and declared that though Persephone must spend six months of every year with Hades in the dark, underground kingdom, the remaining six months she might spend with her mother on the earth.

You may imagine the delight of Demeter when it came time for her daughter to return to her for the first time. She stood anxiously at the door of her cottage, waiting, watching, while the former companions of Persephone stood about where they might welcome her. Suddenly there seemed to be a new freshness in the air; the grass in the meadows, long dry, grew green before their eyes, and purple violets and yellow buttercups started up all about them.

"She is come!" they cried, and sure enough, she was advancing toward them across the meadows, her hands outstretched, her garments blowing in the breeze, no longer the sad, white-faced queen of the underworld, but the old glad Persephone who had left them long before.

## II. THE STORY OF PHAETHON

When the boys with whom Phaethon played about the fields and riverbanks boasted of their fathers, Phaethon was silent. His mother, he knew, was more beautiful than the mothers of his friends; his grandfather was a wealthy, honored man; but his father—he knew nothing whatever about a father. This was bad enough, but when his playmates began to see that such was the fact, they made him suffer constantly.

"No one can play in this game unless he can tell who his father is," one would cry mischievously.

"Let's spend our time telling about the greatest deeds our fathers ever did," another would suggest.

And Phaethon, ashamed and angry, would rush home to his mother and pour out his wrath and shame.

Some day, Phaethon," she would assure him, "you shall know about your father, and then none of the other boys will dare to taunt you."

"But I want to know now!" Phaethon would insist, stamping his foot.

"You are too young yet, my son," Clymene would reply, looking sadly at her son.

At length one day when Phaethon had grown to be a tall, handsome lad, he came into the house in a fiercer state of anger than usual.

I will endure this no longer!" he cried. "Either I shall be able to tell those insulting boys tomorrow who my father is, or I shall never look them in the face again."

Clymene smiled. "Come here Phaethon," she said, "and let me whisper something in your ear."

What he heard made the boy look, first, astonished, then delighted; and he rushed out-of-doors and back to the place where he had left his comrades, radiant with joy.

"*Now* let's tell tales of the deeds of our fathers!" he cried.

And the other boys looked at him in surprise.

"But you have no father," one of them declared.

"O haven't I!" replied Phaethon, no longer angered by the taunt that had so many times stung him. "You see him every day when he drives his chariot across the highest part of the heavens. He is Apollo, the sun god."

A burst of laughter greeted this proud statement.

"Oho!" cried one boy. "Why could you not have made up that story some years ago and saved yourself a great deal of embarrassment?"

"Do you actually expect us to believe that?" asked another, with a sneer.

Disappointed, angry, Phaethon turned again toward home. Having a father was as bad as not having one, if you could not convince other people of his existence.

But his mother was ready to help him out of this

difficulty. Looking at him proudly, she said, "No father would be ashamed to acknowledge you as his son. To-morrow morning you may go to Apollo, and ask him whether what I have told you is not the truth."

The impatient boy could scarcely wait for the morning to come, and long before daybreak, while the stars and moon were still to be seen in the sky, he started off toward the East, traveling as rapidly as he could. At last he came to the gorgeous palace of the Sun and was admitted within the doors to the very throne-room of his father. There, on the diamond-studded throne, sat the radiant god, wearing a purple robe and bearing on his head the crown of beams.

"Who are you," he asked, "who have come here to my palace? It is almost time for me to set out on my day's journey and I have not long to talk with you."

Impulsively Phaethon poured out the story of his wrongs, and ended with a plea that his father would give him some sign by which he might convince his skeptical comrades. Apollo laid aside the beams from about his head, which were so dazzling that the youth could not approach closely, and called the boy to him.

"To be sure you are my son," he declared, "a son whom any father might be proud to own. I am willing to give you any proof of the fact, and I swear by the River Styx (and that is an oath that even the strongest of the gods would not dare to break) that I will grant you any wish that you may ask of me."

This was precisely what Phaethon had hoped for, but had hardly dared to expect, and it did not take him long to give his answer.

"There is one thing," he declared, "that will really be a proof. Let me drive for one day your great chariot across the sky; then no one who sees me can doubt that I am your son."

Now Apollo was very sorry for the rash promise that he had made.

"Choose something else, my son," he begged; "what you have asked for is not safe. You can have no idea of the dangers of the path across the heavens. The road at the beginning of the journey slopes upward so steeply that even my horses can hardly climb it; the middle of the road is so high above the earth that even I, myself, become dizzy when I look down; and the last part of the road slopes downward so rapidly that it is almost impossible to hold in the horses. If it is hard for me, think what it would be for you."

But Phaethon refused to think. He had set his heart on this one thing and this one thing he would have. He knew his father could not break the oath that he had sworn by the River Styx, so he persisted in his demand. At last, attended by the Seasons, the Days, the Months, the Years, and the Hours, Apollo led the way to where the sun chariot stood waiting. It was the most gorgeous chariot that Phaethon had ever looked upon—of gold and silver and precious gems—and his heart beat proudly that he was actually to have the guiding of the magnificent car for a whole day. The horses were led forth and fastened to the chariot, and Eos, the goddess of dawn, threw open the doors of the East, through which the sun in its splendor was presently to rise. After a final plea, which Phaethon stubbornly resisted, Apollo anointed the boy's head with ointment so that he might not be scorched by the brightness of the beams, and then set the crown of rays on the young head.

"Remember, my son," he said, "do not drive too high or too low; a middle course is best. Above all, do not attempt to use the whip, for the horses are spirited; and hold tight to the reins."

Only half heeding his father's instructions, Phaethon sprang into the chariot, grasped the reins, and shaking them over his steeds, started out through the open door.

It did not take the horses long to feel that it was an unpracticed hand that grasped the reins, and, taking the bits in their teeth, they dashed out of the traveled road and wildly up the heavens. The courage with which Phaethon had started out did not last long. Below him—a dizzying, sickening distance below—was the earth and the sea. What if he should drop from this awful height! And there, when he looked about him in the heavens, were even worse sights; the Big Bear and the Little Bear, the Scorpion and the Lion, the huge Crab— all of these seemed to be reaching out toward him as he dashed among them. Up, up, up, went the horses, and then as suddenly downward, almost taking the breath from Phaethon's body with their rapid plunge. They came so close to the earth that mountains that for thousands of years had been snow-crowned lost their snow-caps and stood bare and brown; rivers were dried up; a great part of Africa was burned to a desert; and many of the people were scorched almost black.

Phaethon had long before this dropped the reins,

and he stood shaking with terror. Cries came up to him from the earth, cries of pain and terror and fright from the people of the countries over which he was passing. But he was too much afraid for his own safety to worry about others.

The cries did, however, reach the ears of Zeus, the king of the earth and heavens, where he sat on his throne on Olympus, and he, horrified, looked out upon the course of the wild boy. The other gods and goddesses gathered about him and besought him to save the earth.

"There will be no beauty, no freshness left," they cried. "There will be no cool springs and lakes for the nymphs to live in; no great trees and forests where dryads may shelter themselves."

"I call you all to witness! There is no other way to save the earth but this!" cried Zeus, and he raised his arm and hurled a bolt of lightning at the luckless Phaethon.

Struck from the chariot, the boy fell headlong into a great river, while the horses trotted quietly across the remaining part of their course and disappeared into the doors of the West.

## III. THE STORY OF ARACHNE

Arachne had many things of which she might have been very proud; she was young, beautiful, and had many friends. But she cared less for any of these things than she did or the fact that she was a very skillful weaver. People came from all the country near her home to see the beautiful patterns that she wove on her loom; and as they watched the web grow under her fingers they would exclaim, "Surely Athena herself must have taught you; in no other way could you have learned to do such wonderful work."

Most girls would have been proud to have been taken for a pupil of the wisest and most skillful of the goddesses, but Arachne was so proud that she could not bear to have people think that Athena ever could have taught her anything. Finally her boasts came to the ears of Athena herself. Now, Athena was not naturally cruel or revengeful, but there was a wickedness in any mortal's setting herself up to surpass a deity that even Athena could not pardon. Determined, however, to give the boastful girl a chance, Athena took the form of an old woman and went to Arachne's home.

"Foolish girl," she said, "how do you dare to set yourself up as an equal in skill to the goddess of the arts? Do you not know that she could punish you severely for such boasting?"

"Let her!" said Arachne. "I am her equal, and I am willing that she should know what I have said. Let her come and match her skill with mine—and if I am beaten I will pay the penalty."

"Foolish girl!" cried the goddess, dropping her disguise and appearing in her own radiant form; "the trial shall take place here and now."

All those who stood by were terrified; some of them fell at the feet of Athena; others besought Arachne to yield before it was too late. But the proud girl remained defiant, unafraid.

So the contest began, while the bystanders stood breathless with fear and admiration. Athena at her loom worked rapidly, the shuttle seeming to fly as she passed it back and forth through the threads; and a marvelously beautiful pattern soon began to show itself in the web. But Arachne's web seemed, to those who watched, little, if any, less perfect than that of the goddess herself. Only, what was this that the reckless girl was daring to do? Not content with defying one of the gods, she chose for her subject in the web she was making the faults and failings of the dwellers on Olympus, showing them so clearly that no one could mistake.

Her own web finished, Athena turned and looked at Arachne's. It was wonderful—the goddess could not but admit it to herself. But the presumption! the wickedness of it! thus to hold up the faults of the god before these staring people.

With her shuttle she tore the beautiful web of Arachne from top to bottom, and then turned to the girl herself.

"Your sin merits death," exclaimed the angry goddess, "but death shall not be your portion. Since, however, you have been so fond of weaving, your punishment shall be, that forever and forever you and your descendants shall make your threads and weave your webs. And wherever men see you they shall tear your webs as I have torn this, and shall drive you from them as I drive you from me now."

And touching the girl upon the forehead, she formed her into a spider.

## IV. THE STORY OF PANDORA

In all the beautiful world there were no women — only men, who lived in a state of utter ease. The food that they needed grew ready to their hand on the trees and shrubs; the air was full of the fragrance of flowers, and there was nothing to do all day but to enjoy themselves and exercise their perfect bodies, which had never known a touch of any disease. But the gods in council decided that a vexatious punishment should be sent to man, and that that punishment should be woman. Accordingly, they ordered the artist-god Hephaestus to make one. Very beautiful she was, and the gods took delight in bestowing upon her wonderful gifts. Apollo made her musical, Hermes gave her powers of persuasion, Aphrodite made her lovable, and in the end they called her Pandora, the *all-gifted*.

Hermes, the messenger-god, was commissioned to take the maiden to earth, and to leave her with Epimetheus, brother of Prometheus; and with her was sent a curious box, about the contents of which no word was said. Epimetheus received her gladly—never had he seen so exquisite and so alluring a creature; and all his friends rejoiced in his good fortune, for envy as yet had not entered the world. The songs of Pandora Epimetheus and his friends found more beautiful than the songs of the birds, and they loved to gather about her when the purple twilight was falling and listen to the tales she invented for them.

For a time Pandora was very happy. The world was new and very wonderful, and every day there were countless things to learn. She found out about the mysteries of fire, which looked like a great wind-tossed flower but was so powerful; about the delightful warmth of the day and the delightful cool of the night; about the tastes of the various fruits, all so delicious but all so different. But in the back of her mind there was one persistent, nagging little trouble that grew larger and larger and threatened to spoil all her pleasure. For Hermes had forbidden her, with the sternest words and the severest look, to open the box he had left with Epimetheus, so there was one thing in the world that she could not find out about. And she wanted to know—O, how she wanted to know!

"Probably," she thought, "there are lovely things in the box that would make me even more beautiful—white robes like Hera's, or a golden girdle like that which Aphrodite wears."

Day after day she fretted, and Epimetheus felt the first sadness he had ever known creep over him as he saw Pandora's sadness. Finally she told him what was troubling her, and besought him to open the box; for there was the golden key hanging by a golden cord. But Epimetheus was horrified.

"Do that which the gods have forbidden?" he cried. "Never! The box shall stand in my house forever, and I shall never open it," and he went back to his companions, leaving Pandora to indulge her curiosity alone.

For a time Pandora resisted, but one day when she was left alone in the house the temptation became too strong for her. She slipped the key into the lock, turned it slowly, still but half intending to open it, and then, suddenly, threw back the cover. No beautiful glitter met her eyes, but only a throng of winged pests that buzzed out at her and hurt her with their sharp stings. There was disease in many forms—fever and cholera and rheumatism; there were spite and envy and green-eyed jealousy; there were black worries and gray despairs. She had loosed the ills that were ever after to plague the earth.

In a cloud they swept through the door and windows, darkening the sun, and soon Epimetheus and his companions, at play on a distant green, heard their angry buzzing and felt their stings. And at once dissensions sprang up, and angry words rushed from lips that till now had known only loving ones. Comrade turned upon comrade, and each saw in the other's face his own scowl reflected. The age of innocence had gone, never to return.

Meanwhile at home Pandora sat dismayed. She had slammed down the lid of the box, but too late to shut within it any of the buzzing throng. At length she heard a tiny tapping on the lid, and a tiny voice that said "Let me out! Let me out!"

"No!" she cried. "If there is one of you in there, you shall stay."

But still the tapping and the pleading kept up, and finally Pandora, whose curiosity was not all dead, opened the lid ever so little and peeped in. And there was the most beautiful creature with white wings, which flew merrily out into the light.

"I am Hope, I am Hope," it sang, and it seemed to Pandora that the world grew brighter with its song.

114

Away it flew to the quarreling Epimetheus and his friends, and at its approach the buzzing troubles and wickednesses took their flight, and peace came again. Not the same peace—the peace of innocence had gone forever; but while there was Hope in the world, those men who for the first time had tasted sorrow and anger realized that no troubles would be too bad to be borne.

## V. THE STORY OF ATALANTA

The king of Boeotia had one daughter, Atalanta. While she was more beautiful than any other girl in her father's kingdom, she remained a maiden at home in her father's house, long after all her companions were married. And this was not because she lacked suitors. Young men, handsome, strong, rich, fearless, came constantly to her father's palace, seeking her in marriage, and it was not because the king refused his consent that they went away unhappy.

Atalanta herself was the cause of their unhappiness, for she had made a vow that she would not marry, but would devote her life to the chase, like the goddess Artemis, whom she so much admired. It was hard, however, to be constantly refusing without having any good reason that was apparent, so she made up her mind to give a different answer to her suitors—an answer that would leave no argument. Accordingly, when the next youth presented himself, she replied, "I shall marry the man who can defeat me in a race; but everyone who tries and fails shall be put to death."

This may sound as if Atalanta was a very cruel princess, but her idea was simply to keep people from bothering her with the question of marriage. However, her resolution did not have the effect she expected, for there were still found young men who were anxious enough to have the princess for a wife to submit to the trial that she proposed.

Now, Atalanta could run as swiftly as the deer she hunted in the forests, and however much a youth might pride himself on his speed, he was certain to find it was no match for hers. A number of suitors had met their deaths by reason of their love for her, and the people of her father's kingdom were beginning to murmur among themselves at her cruelty. One day there acted as judge in one of the races a youth, Hippomenes, by name, who had never before seen Atalanta. As he took his place in the judge's seat, he said to himself, looking around at the crowd that had gathered to witness the race, "How can any man be so foolish as to risk his life for the sake of this one girl when there are so many beautiful girls to choose from?"

But when he saw Atalanta step forward, ready for the race, he changed his mind; for never, he felt sure, had he looked upon anything so beautiful, and he found himself hoping that the youths who ran with her would be defeated.

And as she ran she looked even more beautiful. Her bright hair blew backward in the breeze, a lovely color flushed her face and her gracefulness in running was wonderful to look upon. Of course she won, as she always did, and the youths who had made trial of their skill with hers were mercilessly put to death. Even this, however, did not frighten Hippomenes.

"What glory," he said to her, "can there be in defeating weaklings like those who just ran with you? Tomorrow, if you will, I shall try my speed and endurance against yours."

As Atalanta looked at him, she felt that she would scarcely wish to defeat this young man, so handsome did he look, so brave, so worthy to be her partner. Still she only nodded her head and made up her mind that she would give him as hard a trial as she had given the others.

Now, Hippomenes knew, having seen her run, that he could never hope to conquer her in a fair race, but he thought, "There are ways in which it can be managed. Every girl is curious, every girl likes beautiful things."

Accordingly, the next day when he took his place beside Atalanta in the starting line, he had in the front of his robe three beautiful golden apples. As the signal for starting was given, the two sped forward, side by side. For a moment it seemed as if he would actually outrun her, but with a fleet step she passed him. Instantly he seized one of his golden apples and tossed it a little ahead of her. She caught her breath, almost stopped, but her desire to win was strong; however, the beautiful golden sphere looked so tempting that she hastily stooped to grasp it. Running with all his might, Hippomenes threw a second apple, and again Atalanta slacked her speed and seized it, yet kept fairly ahead of her fellow contestant. Almost despairing, Hippomenes tossed slightly to one side of the course the third apple, the largest, ruddiest, most beautiful one of all.

This was too much for the princess. She stopped suddenly, her draperies whirling about her, stooped, and seized the apple. The delay was but for a second, although longer than on the two previous occasions, but that was all Hippomenes needed. He passed her, and with a final rush, reached forward, and touched the maple goal. He had won! and the cheers of the people told that they were glad that at last their beautiful, haughty princess had been conquered.

And as Atalanta came toward Hippomenes and held out the hand in which lay the beautiful golden apples, all could see that she looked far more happy in her defeat than she had ever looked before in all her victories.

# ABOUT THE AUTHOR

Flora J. Cooke (1864–1953) was the first principal of
Chicago's Francis W. Parker School.